JAN 2003

LT Fic
Reid, N
Ethan's
bride /

S0-BFB-859

ETHAN'S
TEMPTRESS BRIDE

ETHAN'S TEMPTRESS BRIDE

BY

MICHELLE REID

MILLS & BOON®

ALAMEDA FREE LIBRARY
2200-A CENTRAL AVENUE
ALAMEDA, CA 94501

All the characters in this book have no existence outside the imagination of the author, and have no relation whatsoever to anyone bearing the same name or names. They are not even distantly inspired by any individual known or unknown to the author, and all the incidents are pure invention.

All Rights Reserved including the right of reproduction in whole or in part in any form. This edition is published by arrangement with Harlequin Enterprises II B.V. The text of this publication or any part thereof may not be reproduced or transmitted in any form or by any means, electronic or mechanical, including photocopying, recording, storage in an information retrieval system, or otherwise, without the written permission of the publisher.

MILLS & BOON and
MILLS & BOON with the Rose Device
are registered trademarks of the publisher.

First published in Great Britain 2002
Large Print edition 2002
Harlequin Mills & Boon Limited,
Eton House, 18-24 Paradise Road,
Richmond, Surrey TW9 1SR

© Michelle Reid 2002

ISBN 0 263 17377 1

Set in Times Roman 16½ on 18 pt.
16-1202-51237

Printed and bound in Great Britain
by Antony Rowe Ltd, Chippenham, Wiltshire

CHAPTER ONE

PARADISE was a sleepy island floating in the Caribbean. It had a bar on the beach, rum on tap and the unique sound of island music, which did seductive things to the hot and humid late afternoon air, while beyond the bar's open rough-wood construction the silky blue ocean lapped lazily against a white-sand shore.

Sitting on a bar stool with a glass of local rum slotted between his fingers, Ethan Hayes decided that it didn't get any better than this. Admittedly it had taken him more than a week to wind down to the point where he no longer itched to reach for a telephone or felt naked in bare feet and shorts instead of sharp suits and highly polished leather shoes. Now he would even go as far as to say that he liked his new laid-back self. 'No worries,' as the locals liked to say, had taken on a whole new meaning for him.

'You want a refill for that, Mr Hayes?' The soft melodic tones of an island accent brought his gaze up to meet that of the beautiful brown girl who was serving behind the bar. Her smile held a different kind of invitation.

'Sure, why not?' He returned a smile and released his glass to her—without acknowledging the hidden offer.

Sex in this hot climate was the serpent in Paradise. As one's body temperature rose, so did that particular appetite, Ethan mused, aware that certain parts of him were suggesting he should consider the offer in the bar-girl's velvet-brown eyes. But he hadn't come to the island to indulge that specific pleasure, and all it took was the tentative touch of a finger to the corner of his mouth to remind him why he was wary of female entanglement. The bruising to his lip and jaw had faded days ago, but the injury to his dignity hadn't. It still throbbed in his breast like an angry tiger in dire need of succour for its nagging wound. If a man had any sense, he wouldn't unleash that tiger on some poor, unsuspecting female; he would keep it severely locked up and avoid temptation at all cost.

Though there was certainly a lot of that about, he acknowledged, as he turned to observe the young woman who was hogging the small bare-board dance floor.

The serpent's mistress, he named her dryly as he watched her sensual undulations to the music. She was a tall and slender toffee-blonde with a perfect Caribbean tan, wearing a short and sassy hot-pink slip-dress that was an almost perfect match for the pink hibiscus flower she wore tucked into her hair.

Eye-catching, in other words. Too irresistible to leave to dance alone, so it wasn't surprising that the young men in the bar were lining up to take their turn with her. She had class, she had style, she had beauty, she had grace, and she danced like a siren, shifting from partner to partner with the ease of one who was used to taking centre stage. Her eager young cohorts were enjoying themselves, loving the excuse to get up close and personal, lay their hands on her sensational body and gaze into big green beautiful eyes or watch her lovely mouth break into a smile that promised them everything.

And her name was Eve. Eve as in temptress, the ruin of man.

Or in this case the ruin of these brave young hunters who were aspiring to be her Adam. For she was the It girl on this small Caribbean island, the girl with everything, one of the fortunate few. A daddy's girl—though in this case it was Grandpa's girl, and the sole heir to his fabulous fortune.

Money was one hell of an aphrodisiac, Ethan decided cynically. Make her as ugly as sin and he could guarantee that those same guys would still be worshipping at her dainty dancing feet. But as so often was the way for the fabulously wealthy, stunning beauty came along with this package.

She began to laugh; the sound was soft and light and appealingly pleasant. She pouted at her present young hunter and almost brought the poor fool to his knees. Then she caught Ethan's eyes on her and the cynical look he was wearing on his face. Her smile withered to nothing. Big green come-and-get-me-if-you-dare eyes widened to challenge his cynicism outright. She knew him, he knew her. They had met several times over the last year at her grandfather's home in Athens, Ethan in his professional role as a design-and-build architect renowned for his creative genius for making new holiday complexes blend into their native surroundings, Eve in her only role as her grandfather's much loved, much spoiled, gift from the gods.

They did not like each other. In fact mutual antipathy ran in a constant stream between them. Ethan did not like her conceited belief that she had been put on this earth to be worshipped by all, and Eve did not like his outright refusal to fall at her feet. So it was putting it mildly to say that it was unfortunate they should both find themselves holidaying in the same place. The island was small enough for them to be thrown into each other's company too often for the comfort of either. Sparks tended to fly, forcing hostility to raise its ugly head. Other people picked up on it and didn't know what to do or say to lighten the atmosphere. Ethan usually solved the problem by withdrawing from the conflict with excuses that he had to be somewhere else.

This time he withdrew by turning away from her, back to the bar and the drink that had just been placed in front of him. But Eve's image remained standing right there, dancing on the bar top. Proud, defiant, unashamedly provocative—doing things to other parts of him he did not want her to reach.

His serpent in paradise, he grimly named this hot and nagging desire he suffered for Theron Herakleides' tantalising witch of a granddaughter.

Eve was keeping a happy smile fixed on her face even if it killed her to do it. She despised Ethan Hayes with an absolute vengeance. He made her feel spoiled and selfish and vain. She wished he had done his usual thing of getting up and walking out, so that she wouldn't have to watch him flirt with the barmaid.

Didn't Ethan know he was treading on dangerous ground there, and that the barmaid's strapping great sailor of a lover would chew him up and spit him out if he caught him chatting up his woman? Or was it the girl who was doing the chatting up? Then Eve had to settle for that as the more probable alternative, because Ethan Hayes was certainly worth the effort.

Great body, great looks, great sense of presence, she listed reluctantly. In a sharp suit and tie he was dynamic and sleek; now simple beach shorts and a white tee shirt should have turned him into something else entirely, but didn't—dynamic and sleek still did it for her, Eve decided as she ran her eyes over him. She began at his brown bare feet with their long toes that were curling lovingly round one of the bar stool crossbars, then moved onwards, up powerfully built legs peppered with dark hair that had been bleached golden by the sun.

How did she know the sun had bleached those hairs? Eve asked herself. Because she'd seen his legs before—had seen *all* of Ethan Hayes before!—on that terrible night at her grandfather's house in Athens, when she'd dared to walk uninvited into his bedroom and had caught him in a state of undress.

Prickly heat began to chase along to her nerve ends at the memory—the heat of mortification, not attraction though the attraction had always been there as well. She had gone to Ethan's room to confront him over something he had seen her doing in the garden with Aidan Galloway. Bristling with self-righteous indignation she had marched in through his door, only to stop dead with her head wiped clean of all coherent thought when she'd found him standing there still dripping water from a recent shower, and as stark staring naked as a man could be—not counting the small hand towel he had been using to dry his hair. The towel had quickly covered other parts of him, but not before she'd had a darn good owl-eyed look!

Oh, the shame, the embarrassment! She could feel her cheeks blushing even now. 'I presume Mr Galloway ran back to his fiancée, so you thought you would come and try your luck here.' Eve winced as Ethan's cutting words came back to slay her all over again.

'Your foot, sorry,' her present dance partner apologised.

He had misinterpreted the wince. 'That's okay,' she said, smiling sweetly at Raoul Delacroix without bothering to correct his mistake—and wished she'd had the wits to smile sweetly at Ethan Hayes that night, instead of running like a fool and leaving him with *his* mistake!

But she had run without saying a single word to him in her own defence, and by the next morning embarrassment had turned to stiff-necked pride; hell could freeze over before she would explain anything to him! As a result he had become the conscience she knew she did not deserve, because all it took was a glance from those horribly critical grey eyes to make her feel crushingly guilty!

It wasn't fair, she hated him for it. Hated his dark good looks too because they did things to her she would rather they didn't. But most of all she hated his cold, grim, English reserve that kept him forever at a distance, thereby stopping her from beginning the confrontation that she knew would completely alter his perception of her.

Did she need to do that? Eve asked herself suddenly. And was horrified to realise how badly she did.

'Have dinner with me tonight...' Her present dance partner was suddenly crowding her with his too eager hands and the fervent darkening of his liquid brown eyes. 'Just the two of us,' Raoul huskily extended. 'Somewhere quiet and romantic where no one can interrupt.'

'You know that's a no-no, Raoul.' Smiling to soften the refusal, she also deftly dislodged one of his hands from her rear. 'We're here as a group to have fun, not romance.'

'Romance can be fun.' His rejected hand lifted up to brush a finger across her bottom lip with a message only a very naïve woman would misinterpret.

Eve reached up and firmly removed the finger and watched his beautifully shaped mouth turn down in a sulk. Raoul Delacroix was a very handsome French-American, with eyes dark enough to drown in and a body to die for—yet he did nothing for her. In a way she wished that he did because he was her age and her kind of person, unlike the disapproving Ethan Hayes who added a whole new meaning to the phrase, the generation gap.

And what was that gap—her twenty-three years to his thirty-seven? Big gap—yawning gap, she mocked it dryly. 'Don't sulk,' she scolded Raoul. 'Today is my birthday and we're supposed to be having lots of fun.'

'Tomorrow is your birthday,' he corrected.

'As we all know, my grandfather is arriving here tomorrow to help me celebrate, which means I will have to behave with proper decorum all day. So tonight we agreed that we would celebrate my birthday a day early. Don't spoil that for me, Raoul.'

It was both a gentle plea and a serious warning because he had been getting just a little bit too intense recently. Raoul Delacroix was the half-brother of André Visconte who owned the only hotel on the island. So like the rest of the crowd whose families owned property here, they'd all been meeting up for holidays since childhood. They were all good close friends now who'd agreed early on that romance would spoil what they enjoyed most about each others' company. Raoul knew the rules, so attempting to change them now was just a tiny bit irritating—and a shame because he was usually very good company—when he wasn't thinking of other things, that was.

'The beach is strewn with good prospects for a handsome Frenchman to play the romantic,' she teased him. 'Take your pick. I can guarantee they will swoon at your feet.'

'I know, I've tried one or two,' Raoul returned lazily. 'But this was only in practice, you understand,' he then added, 'to prepare myself for the woman I love.'

Implying that Eve was that woman? She laughed, it was so funny. After a moment, Raoul joined in the laughter, and the mood between them relaxed back into being playful. The music changed not long after, calypso taking the place of reggae, and Eve found Raoul's place taken by another admirer while he moved on to pastures new.

Viewing this little by-play via the mirror on the wall behind the drinks optics, Ethan wasn't sure he liked the expression on Raoul Delacroix's face as he'd turned away from Eve. Raoul's look did nasty things to Ethan's insides and made him curious as to what Raoul and Eve had been talking about. They'd parting laughing, but Raoul's turning expression had been far from amused.

None of your business, he then told himself firmly. Eve knew what kind of dangerous game she was playing with all of these testosterone-packed young men. My God, did she know, he then added with a contempt that went so deep it reflected clearly on his face when, as if on cue, Aidan Galloway walked into the bar. The darkly attractive young Irish-

American paused, found his target and made directly for Eve.

The last time Ethan had seen Aidan Galloway had been a month ago in Athens when he had been a guest of Eve's grandfather, along with several members of the Galloway family. On the face of it, the younger man had only had eyes for the beautiful fiancée he'd had hanging from his arm. But since coming to this island, Ethan had seen no sign of the fiancée and Aidan Galloway now only had eyes for Eve.

Someone slid onto the stool next to him, offering him a very welcome alternative to observing the life and loves of Eve Herakleides. It was Jack Banning who managed the only hotel on the island for owner, André Visconte. Jack was a big all-American guy, built to break rocks against but as laid-back as they came.

'Marlin have been spotted five miles out,' Jack informed him. 'I'm taking a boat out tomorrow. If you're interested in some big-game fishing, you're welcome to come.'

'Early start?' Ethan quizzed.

'Think sunrise,' Jack suggested. 'Think deep yawns and black coffee and no heavy partying the night before if you don't want to spend your time at sea throwing up.'

The barmaid interrupted by appearing with a glass of rum for Jack. The two of them chatted boss to employee for a few minutes, but the girl's eyes kept on drifting towards Ethan, and when she had moved away again Jack sent Ethan a very male glance.

'Considering a different kind of game?' Jack posed lazily.

'Not today, thanks.' Ethan's smile was deliberately benign as he took a sip at his drink.

'Or any day that you've been here, from what my sources say.'

'Was that an idle question or a veiled criticism of my use of the island's rich and varied hospitality?'

'Neither.' A set of even white teeth appeared to acknowledge Ethan's sarcastic hit. 'It was just an observation. I mean—look at you, man,' Jack mocked him. 'You've got the looks, you've got the body parts, and I know for a fact that you've had more than one lovely woman's heart fluttering with anticipation since you arrived, but I've yet to see you take a second look at any of them.'

He was curious. Ethan didn't entirely blame him. The island was not sold on its monastic qualities. The women here were, in the main, beautiful people and a lot of them had made it clear that they were available for a little holiday romance.

But Ethan was off romance, off women, and most definitely off sex—or at least he was in training to be off it, he amended, all too aware that his body was trying to tempt him with every inviting smile that came his way.

Then there was that other sexual temptation, the one that hit him hard in his nether regions every time he looked at Eve Herakleides and recalled an incident when she'd walked into his room to find him standing there naked. She'd looked—no *stared*—and things had happened to him that he hadn't experienced since he'd been a hormone-racked teenager. What was worse than the reaction was knowing she'd witnessed it.

So why his eyes had to pick that precise moment to glance in the mirror was something he preferred not to analyse. She was dancing with Aidan Galloway, and the body language was nothing like what it had been when she'd danced with the other men. No, this was tense, it was serious. It reminded him of that kiss he had witnessed in her grandfather's garden in Athens. The two of them had been so engrossed in each other that they hadn't heard his arrival—nor had they known they'd also been watched by Aidan's fiancée, who'd almost fainted into the arms of another young Galloway.

Eve was a flirt and a troublemaker, a woman with no scruples when it came to other women's men. Her only mission in life was to slay all with those big green you-can-have-me eyes.

Ethan loved those eyes...

The unexpected thought jolted him, snapped his gaze down from the mirror to his glass. What the hell is the matter with you? he asked himself furiously. Too much sun? Too much time on your hands? Maybe it was time he got back into a suit and unearthed a mobile telephone.

'And you?' He diverted his attention back to Jack Banning. 'Do you sip the honey on a regular basis here?'

Jack gave a rueful shake of his head. 'The boss would have my balls for trophies if I imbibed,' he murmured candidly. 'No...' picking up his glass he tasted the rum '...I have this lovely widow living on the next island who keeps me sane in that department.'

With no ties, and no commitment expected or desired, Ethan concluded from that, knowing the kind of woman Jack was talking about because he'd enjoyed a few of them himself in his time.

'She's a good woman,' Jack added as if he needed to make that point.

'I don't doubt it,' Ethan replied, and he didn't. In the time he had been here, he had got to know and like Jack Banning. Being in the leisure business himself—though in a different area—he wasn't surprised that André Visconte had a man like Jack in place. In fact he was considering doing a bit of head-hunting because they could do with Jack running the new resort his company was in the process of constructing in Spain.

Though that idea was shot to pieces when Jack spoke again. 'Her husband was caught out at sea in a hurricane four years ago,' he said quietly. 'He left her well shod but heavily pregnant. Left her with a badly broken heart too.'

Which told Ethan that Jack was in love with the widow. Which in turn meant there was no hope of getting him to leave for pastures new.

'So what's your excuse for the self-imposed celibacy?' Jack asked curiously.

Same as you, Ethan thought grimly. I fell for a married woman—only her husband is very much alive and kicking. 'Too much of a good thing is reputed to be bad for you,' was what he offered as a dry reply.

Glancing at him, he saw Jack's gaze touch that part of Ethan's jaw where the bruising had been obvious a few days ago. He had been forced to wear the mark like a banner when he'd first arrived on the island. Speculation as to how he'd received the bruise had been rife. His refusal to discuss it had only helped to fire people's imagination.

But the expression in Jack's eyes told him that Jack had drawn a pretty accurate conclusion. He sighed, so did Jack. Both men lifted their glass to their mouths and said no more. It had been that kind of conversation: some things had been said, others not, but all had been taken on board nonetheless. Turning on his stool, Jack offered the busy bar room a once-over with his lazy-yet-shrewd manager's eye, while Ethan studied the contents of his glass with a slightly bitter gaze. He was thinking of a woman with dark red hair, silk-white skin and a broken heart that was in the process of being mended by the wrong man, as far as he was concerned.

But the right man for her, he had to add honestly, felt the tiger stir within and wished he knew of a good cure for unrequited love.

'Try the sex,' Jack said suddenly as if he could read his mind. 'It has to be a better option than lusting after the unattainable.'

Unable to restrain it, Ethan released a hard laugh. 'Is that advice for me or for yourself?'

'You,' Jack answered. Then he grimaced as he added, 'Mine is a hopeless case. You see, the widow's son calls me Daddy.' With that he got up and gave Ethan's shoulder a man-to-man, sympathetic pat. 'Let me know about the Marlin trip,' he said and strolled away.

Turning to watch him go, Ethan saw Jack stop once or twice to chat to people on his way out of the bar. One woman in particular came to meet him. It was Eve the temptress. A quick look around and he found Aidan Galloway standing at the other end of the bar. He was ordering a drink and he didn't look happy. Join the club, Ethan thought, as his eyes then picked out Raoul Delacroix who was watching Eve with an expression on his face that matched Aidan Galloway's.

As for Eve, her long slender arms were around Jack's neck and she was pouting up at him in a demand for a kiss. Amiably Jack gave it and smiled at whatever it was she was saying to him. Without much tempting she managed to urge the manager into motion to the music, his big hands spanning her tiny waist, his dark head dipped to maintain eye contact. Like that, they teased each other as they swayed.

Suddenly Ethan knew it was time to leave. Downing the rest of his drink, he came to his feet, placed some money on the bar and wished the girl behind it a light farewell. As he walked towards the dancers he thought he saw Eve move that extra inch closer to Jack's impressive body.

Done for his benefit? he asked himself, then shot that idea in the foot with a silent huff of scorn to remind himself that Eve Herakleides disliked him as much as he disliked her.

Outside the air was like warm damp silk against his skin. The humidity was high, and looking out to sea Ethan could see clouds gathering on the horizon aiming to spoil the imminent sunset. There could be a storm tonight, he predicted as he turned in the direction of his beach house. Behind him the sound of a woman's laughter came drifting towards him from inside the bar. Without thinking he suddenly changed direction and his feet were kicking hot sand as he ran toward the water and made a clean racing dive into its cool clear depths.

'Don't even think about it,' Jack cautioned. 'He's too old and too dangerous for a sweet little flirt like you.'

Dragging her eyes away from the sight of Ethan Hayes in full sprint as he headed for the ocean, Eve looked into Jack Banning's knowing gaze—and mentally ran for cover. 'I don't know what you're talking about,' she said.

Jack didn't believe her. 'Ethan Hayes could eat you for a snack without touching his appetite,' he informed her without a hint of mockery to make the bitter pill of truth an easier one to swallow.

'Like you, you mean,' she said with a kissable pout, which was really another duck-and-run. 'Big bad Jack,' she murmured as she moved in closer then began swaying so provocatively that he had to physically restrain her.

He did it with a white-toothed, highly amused, grin. 'Minx,' he scolded. 'If your grandfather could see you he would have you locked up—these messages you put out are dangerous.'

'My grandpa adores me too much to do anything so primitive.'

'Your grandfather, my little siren, arrives on this island tomorrow,' Jack reminded her. 'Let him see this look you're wearing on your face and we will soon learn how primitive he can be...'

CHAPTER TWO

ETHAN took his time swimming down the length of the bay to come out of the water opposite the beach house he was using while he was here. It belonged to Leandros Petronades, a business associate, who had understood his need to get away from it all for a week or two if he wasn't going to do something stupid like walk out on his ten-year-strong working partnership with Victor Frayne.

Victor... Ethan's feet stilled at the edge of the surf as the same anger that had caused the rift between the two of them rose up to burn at his insides again.

Victor had used him, or had allowed him to be used, as a decoy in the crossfire between Victor's daughter, Leona, and her estranged husband, Sheikh Hassan Al-Qadim. In the Sheikh's quest to recover his wife, Leona and Ethan had been ambushed then dragged off into the night. When Ethan had eventually come round from a knockout blow to his jaw,

27

it had been to find he'd been made virtual prisoner on Sheikh Hassan's luxury yacht. But if he'd thought his pride had taken a battering when he'd been wrestled to the ground and rendered helpless with that knockout blow, then his interview with the Sheikh the next morning had turned what was left of his pride to pulp.

The man was an arrogant bastard, Ethan thought grimly. What Leona loved about him he would never understand. If *he* had been her father, he would have been putting up a wall of defence around her rather than aiding and abetting her abduction by a man whom everyone knew had been about to take a second wife!

Leona had been out of that marriage—*best* out of that marriage! Now she was back in it with bells ringing and—

Bending down he picked up a conch shell then turned and hurled it into the sea. He wished to goodness he hadn't had that conversation with Jack Banning. He wished he could stuff all of these violent feelings back into storage where he had managed to hide them for the last week. Now he was angry with himself again, angry with Victor, and angry with Sheikh Hassan Al-Qadim and the whole damn world, probably.

On that heavily honest assessment, he turned back to face land again. Leandros Petronades had been his saviour when he'd offered him the use of this place. Not that the Greek's motives had been in the least bit altruistic, Ethan reminded himself. As one of the main investors in their Spanish project, Leandros had been protecting his own back, plus several other business ventures his company had running with Hayes-Frayne. A bust up between Ethan and Victor would have left him with problems he did not need or want. So when he'd happened to walk in on the furious row the two partners had been locked in, had seen the huge purple bruise on Ethan's face and had heard enough to draw his own conclusions as how the bruise got there, Leandros had immediately suggested that Ethan needed a break while he cooled off.

So here he was, standing on the beach of one of the most exclusive islands in the Caribbean, and about the lush green hillside in front of him nestled the kind of properties most

people only dreamed about. The Visconte hotel complex occupied a central position, forming the hub around which all activities on the
island revolved. Either side of the hotel stood
the private villas belonging to those wealthy
enough to afford a plot of land here. André
Visconte himself owned a private estate. The
powerful Galloway family owned many properties, forming a small hamlet of their own in
the next bay. But if the size of a plot was in-
dicative of wealth, then the villa belonging to
Theron Herakleides had to be the king.

Painted sugar-pink, it sat inside a framework
of ancient date- and fabulous flame-trees about
halfway up the hill. From the main house the
garden swept down to sea level via a series of
carefully tended terraces: sun terraces, pool
terraces, garden terraces that wouldn't be believed to be real outside a film set. There were
tennis courts and even a velvet smooth croquet
lawn, though Ethan could not bring himself to
imagine that Theron Herakleides had ever
bothered to use it. Then there were the guest
houses scattered about the grounds, all painted
that sugar-pink colour which came into its own
with every burning sunset. Almost on the sand

sat the Herakleides beach house, the part of her grandfather's estate that Eve was using while she was here.

It had to be the worst kind of luck that the Petronades and the Herakleides estates were beside each other, because it placed her beach house right next door to his, Ethan mused heavily, as he trod the soft sand on his way up the beach. Other than for Eve's close proximity he was happy with his modest accommodation. The beach houses might be small but they possessed a certain charm that appealed to the artist in him. Nothing grand: just an open-plan living room and kitchen, a bathroom and a bedroom.

All he needed, in other words, he acknowledged as he came to a stop at the low whitewashed wall that was there to help keep the sand back rather than mark the boundary to the property. Set into the wall was a white picket gate that gave access to a simple garden and the short path that led to a shady veranda. Next to the gate was a concrete tub overhung by a freshwater shower head. Pulling his wet tee shirt off over his head he tossed it onto the wall, then stepped into the tub and switched on the tap that brought cool water cascading over his head.

His skin shone dark gold in the deepening sunset, muscles rippled across his shoulders and back, as he sluiced the sand and salt from his body. Standing a few short yards away on the hot concrete path that ran right around the bay, Eve watched him with the same fascination she had surrendered to the last time she had chanced upon Ethan Hayes like this.

Only it wasn't the same, she reminded herself quickly. He was dressed, or that part of him which caused her the most problems was modestly covered at least. But as for the rest of him—

Water ran off his dark hair down his face to his shoulders. The hair on his chest lay matted in thick coils that arrowed down to below his waist. She hadn't noticed the chest hair the last time—hadn't noticed the six-pack firmness of his abdomen. He was lean and he was tight and he was honed to perfection, and she wished she—

'You can go past. I won't bite,' the man himself murmured flatly, letting her know that he had seen her standing here.

Fingers curling into two fists at her sides, Eve released a soft curse beneath her breath. I hate him, she told herself. I *really* hate him for catching me doing this, not once but *twice!*

'Actually I quite like the view,' she returned, determined not to let him embarrass her a second time. 'You strip down quite nicely for an Englishman.'

More muscles flexed; Eve's lungs stopped working. She wished she understood this fascination she had for his body, but she didn't. She could not even say that he possessed the best body she had ever seen—mainly because it was the *only* one she had seen in its full and flagrant entirety. That, she decided, had to be the cause of this wicked fascination she had for Ethan Hayes. It fizzed through her veins like a champagne cocktail, stripped her mouth of moisture like crisp dry wine. Tantalising, in other words. The man was a stiff-necked, supercritical, overbearing boor, yet inside she fluttered like a love-struck teenager every time she saw him.

The shower was turned off. He threw one of those cold-eyed looks at her then slid it away without saying a word. He was going to do his usual thing and walk away as if she didn't exist, Eve realised, and suddenly she was determined to break that arrogant habit for good!

'You've missed a bit,' she informed him.

He turned a second look on her. Looks like that could kill, Eve thought as, with a scrupulously bland expression, she pointed to the back of his legs where beautifully pronounced calf muscles were still peppered with fine granules of sand.

Still without saying a word he turned on the shower again. A sudden urge to laugh brought Eve's ready sense of humour into play and she decided to have a bit of fun at the stuffy Ethan Hayes' expense.

'Jack just warned me off falling for you,' she announced, watching him wash the sand off his legs. 'He thinks you're dangerous. The eat-them-for-a   snack-as-you-walk-out-of-the-door kind of man.'

'Wise man, Jack.' She thought she heard him mutter over the splash of water, but she couldn't be sure.

'I laughed because I thought it was so funny,' she went on. 'I mean—we both know you're too much the English gentleman to do anything so crass as to love them and leave them without a backward glance.'

It was not a compliment and Ethan didn't take it as one. 'You keep taking a dig at my Englishness, but you're half English yourself,' he pointed out.

'I know.' Eve sighed with mocking tragedy. 'It worries the Greek in me sometimes that I could end up falling for a die-hard English stuffed-shirt.'

'Fate worse than death.'

'Yes.'

He switched the shower off again and Eve rediscovered her fascination with his body as he turned to recover his wet tee shirt; muscles wrapped in rich brown flesh rippled in the red glow of the sunlight, droplets of water clung to the hairs on his chest.

Ethan turned to catch her staring. The prickling sensation between his thighs warned him that he had better get away from here before he embarrassed himself again. Yet he didn't move, couldn't seem to manage the simple act. His senses were too busy drinking in what his eyes were showing him. He liked the way she was wearing her hair twisted cheekily up on her head with a hibiscus flower helping to hold it in place. He liked what the pink dress did for her figure and the slender length and shape of her legs. And he liked her mouth; it was heart-shaped—small with a natural provocative yen to pout. He liked her smooth golden skin, her cute little nose, and those eyes that had a way of looking at him as if she...

Go away, Eve, he wanted to say to her. Instead he dragged his eyes away, and looked for something thoroughly innocuous to say. 'I thought you were all off to a party this evening.' Flat-voiced, level-toned, he'd thought he'd hit innocuous perfectly.

But Eve clearly didn't. She stiffened up as if he had just insulted her. 'Oh, do let's be honest and call it an orgy,' she returned. 'Since you believe that orgies are more my style.'

Time to go, he decided, and opened the picket gate.

'While you do what you're probably very good at, of course,' she added, 'and play whist with the cheese and wine set at the hotel.'

He went still.

Eve's heart stopped beating on the suspicion that she had finally managed to rouse the sleeping tiger she'd always fancied lurked within his big chest. Sometimes—usually when she was least expecting it—Ethan Hayes could take on a certain quality that made her think of dangerous animals. This was one of those times, and her biggest problem was that she liked it—it excited her.

'How old are you?' he asked.

He knew exactly how old she was. 'Twenty-three until midnight,' she told him anyway.

He nodded his wet head. 'That accounts for it.'

This was blatant baiting, Eve recognised, and foolishly took it. 'Accounts for what?'

'The annoyingly adolescent desire to insult and shock.'

He was so right, but oh, it hurt. Why had she willingly let herself fall into that? Eve had no defence, none at all and she had to turn to stare out to sea so that he wouldn't see the sudden flood of weak tears that were trying to fill her eyes.

And who was the adolescent who made that cutting comment? Ethan was grimly asking himself, as he looked at her standing there looking like an exotic flower that had been cut down in its prime. Oh, damn it, he thought, and walked through the gate, meaning to get the hell away from this before he—

He couldn't do it. Muscles were tightening all over his body on wave after wave of angry guilt. What had she ever done to him after all? If you didn't count a couple of teasing come-ons and letting him catch her in a heated clinch with someone else's man.

She'd also caught him naked and had had a full view of his embarrassing response, but he didn't want to think about that. Instead he took in a deep breath and spun back to say something trite and stupid and hopefully less—

But he found he was too late because she had already walked off, a tall slender figure with a graceful stride and a proud yet oddly vulnerable tilt to her head. Still cursing himself for the whole stupid conversation, Ethan made himself walk up the path. Though, as he reached the shade of the veranda, he couldn't resist a quick glance sideways and saw Eve was about to enter her house. One part of him wanted to go after her and apologise, but the major part told him wisely to leave well alone.

Eve Herakleides could mean trouble if he allowed himself to be sucked in by her frankly magnetic appeal. He didn't need that kind of stimulation. He didn't want to end up in the same fated boat he had been in before with a woman just like her.

What was it that Jack had called it? 'Lusting after the unattainable.' Eve was destined to higher things than a mere architect had to offer—as her grandfather would be happy to tell him. But it was the word lust that made Ethan go inside and firmly close his door.

CHAPTER THREE

EVE tried to enjoy the party. In fact she threw herself into the role of life and soul with an enthusiasm that kept everyone else entertained.

But the scene with Ethan Hayes had taken the edge off her desire to enjoy anything tonight. And she was worried about Aidan. He had been drinking steadily since he'd arrived at the bar on the beach late this afternoon and his mood suited the grim compulsion with which he was pouring the rum down his throat.

Not that anyone else seemed to have noticed, she realised, as she watched him do his party trick with a cocktail shaker and bottle of something very green to the laughing encouragement of the rest of the crowd, whereas she felt more like weeping.

For Aidan—for herself? In truth, she wasn't quite sure. On that low note she surrendered to the deep doldrums that had been dogging her every movement tonight and slid open one of the glass doors that led onto the terrace.

Then she stepped out into the warm dark night, intending to walk across the decking to the terrace rail that overlooked the sea—only it came as a surprise to discover that she was ever so slightly tipsy, so tipsy in fact that she was forced to sink onto the first sunbed she reached just in case she happened to fall down.

Well, why not? she thought with a little shrug, and slipping off her shoes she lifted her feet up onto the cool, cushioned mattress, then relaxed against the raised chair back with a low long sigh. The air was soft and seductively quiet, the earlier threatened storm having passed them by. Reclining there, she listened to the low slap of lazy waves touching the shore, and wondered dully how much longer she needed to leave it before she could escape to brood on her own terrace without inviting comment here?

At least Aidan was already in the right place for when he eventually sank into a drunken stupor, she mused heavily. This was his home, or the one he liked to call home of several the family had dotted around this tiny bay. With a bit of luck he was going to slide under a convenient table soon and she could get some of the guys to put him to bed, then forget about him and his problems for a while and concentrate on her own.

She certainly had a few, Eve acknowledged through the mud of her half-tipsy state. Ethan Hayes and his horrible attitude towards her was one of them. Her grandfather in his whole, sweet, bullying entirety was another. The older he got, the more testy he became, and more determined to run her life for her. She smiled as she thought that about him though, and allowed her mind to drift back to the last conversation she'd had with him over the phone before she'd flown out here from her London flat.

'Grandpa, will you stop trying to marry me off to every eligible man you happen to meet?' she scolded, 'I am only twenty-three years' old, for goodness' sake!'

'At twenty-three you should be suckling my first grandson at your breast while the next grows big in your belly,' he complained.

'Barefoot I presume, while making baklava for my very fat husband.'

Eve hadn't been able to resist it, she chuckled into the night at the outrageous scenario.

'Spiridon is not fat.'

'But he is twice my age.'

'He is thirty-nine,' the old man corrected. 'Very handsome. Very fit. The ladies worship him.'

'And you ought to be ashamed of yourself for trying to foist me off with the most notorious rake in Greece,' she rebuked. 'I thought you loved me better than this.'

'You are the unblemished golden apple of my eye!' Theron Herakleides announced with formidable passion. 'I merely want you to remain that way until I see you safely married before I die.'

'Die?' she repeated. He was bringing out the big guns with that remark. 'Now listen to me, you scheming old devil,' she scolded, 'I love you to bits. *You* are the love of my life! But if you stick one—*just one*—eligible man in front of me I will never speak to you again—understand?'

'*Ne,*' the old man answered, gruff-voiced and tetchy. 'Yes, I understand that you bully a sick and lonely old man.'

Sick, she did not believe, but lonely she did. 'See you soon, Grandpa,' she softly ended the conversation.

And she would do—sooner than she'd thought too—because her grandfather was making a flying visit here tomorrow just to spend her birthday with her. The prospect softened her whole face. She loved that stubborn, bad tempered old man almost to distraction. He had been both her mother and father for so many years now that she could barely recall the time when she hadn't looked to him for every little thing she might need.

But not a husband, she quickly reminded herself. That was one decision in her life out of which he was going to have to learn to keep his busy nose!

Why a sudden image of Ethan Hayes had to flash across her eyes at that moment, Eve refused to analyse, but it put a dark frown upon her face.

'Here, try this...' Glancing up she found Raoul Delacroix standing beside her holding out a tall glass full of a pinkish liquid decorated with just about everything, from a selection of tropical fruit pieces to several fancy cocktail sticks and straws.

'What's in it?' she asked warily.

'Aidan called it tiger juice with a bite,' Raoul replied.

Tiger juice, how appropriate, Eve mused dryly, thinking of Ethan Hayes again.

'I'm game, if you are,' Raoul said, bringing her attention to the other glass of the same he was holding. 'It might help take the scowl from your face that you seem to have been struggling with all evening.'

Had her bad mood been that apparent? Eve accepted the glass without further comment, but as Raoul lowered himself onto the sunbed next to hers, she felt a fizz of anger begin to bubble inside because she knew whose fault it was that she was feeling like this!

If she didn't watch out, Ethan Hayes could be in danger of becoming an obsession.

'*Salute.*' Raoul's glass touching the edge of hers brought her mind swinging back to where it should be.

'Cheers,' she replied, unearthed a curly straw from the rest of the pretty junk decorating the glass, put it to her lips and sucked defiantly.

The drink tasted a little strange but not horribly so. She looked at Raoul, he looked at her. 'What do you think?' she asked him curiously.

'Sexy,' he murmured with a teasingly lecherous grin. 'I can feel my toes tingling. I will now encourage the sensation to reach other parts.' With that he took another pull on his straw.

Laughing at his outrageousness, Eve did the same, and it became a challenge as to which of them could empty the glass of Aidan's wicked brew first. After that she remembered little. Not the glass being rescued from her clumsy fingers nor the light-hearted banter that went on around her as the rest of the crowd discussed where the birthday girl should be placed to sleep it off. Aidan offered a bed, someone else suggested she was perfectly fine where she was. Raoul reminded them that her grandfather was due in on the dawn flight, so maybe the wisest place for him to find her tomorrow was in her own bed. This drew unilateral agreement because no one wanted to explain to Theron Herakleides why his precious granddaughter had been so rolling drunk she hadn't even made it home. Raoul offered to deliver her there since it was on the way to his villa, and he'd only had one glass of alcohol.

Everyone agreed because no one else felt sober enough to make the drive.

It was all very relaxed, very light-hearted. No one thought of questioning Raoul's motives as they watched him carry Eve to his car. They were all such long-standing friends after all. All for one, one for all.

CHAPTER FOUR

ETHAN came shooting out of a deep sleep to the sound of a woman's shrill cry. Lying there in his bed with his heart pounding in his chest he listened for a few moments, uncertain that it hadn't been someone screaming in his dream.

Then the second cry came, and he was rolling out of bed and landing on his feet before the sound had come to a chillingly abrupt halt. Grabbing up a pair of beach shorts he pulled them on, then began moving fast out of his bedroom, across the sitting room and through the front door, where he paused to look around for some clue as to where the cries had come from.

It was pitch black outside and whisper-quiet; nothing stirred—even the ocean was struggling to make a sound as it lapped the shore. Peering out towards the sea, he was half expecting to see someone in difficulties out there, but no flailing silhouette broke the moon-dusted surface. The cries had been close—much closer to house than the water.

Then it came again, and even as he swung round to face Eve's beach house he saw the shadowy figure of a man slink down the veranda steps.

Eve was the screamer. His heart began to thump. 'Hey—!' he called out, startling the figure to a standstill halfway down the veranda steps. It was too dark to get a clear look at him but Ethan had his suspicions. He sure did have those, he thought grimly, as he began striding towards the boundary wall that separated the two properties. The name Aidan Galloway was burning like a light bulb inside his head. 'What the hell is going on?' he demanded, only to prompt the other man to turn and make a sudden run for it.

His skin began to crawl with a sense that something was really wrong here. People didn't run unless they had a reason to. Thinking no further than that, he gave chase, sprinting across the dry spongy grass and vaulting the wall without even noticing. Within seconds the figure had disappeared around the corner of Eve's beach house. By the time Ethan rounded that corner all he saw were the red tail-lights of a car taking off up the narrow lane which gave access to the beach from the road above.

On a soft curse he then turned his thoughts to Eve. Spinning about, he stepped onto her veranda and began striding along its cool tiled surface until he came to the door. It was swinging wide on its hinges and he stepped warily through it into complete darkness.

'Eve—?' he called out. 'Are you all right?'

He received no answer.

'Eve—!' he called again, more sharply this time.

Still no reply came back at him. He had never been in here before so he had to strain his eyes to pick out the shapes of walls and pieces of furniture as he began moving forwards. He bumped into something hard, found himself automatically reaching out to steady a table lamp by its shade and had the foresight to switch it on. Light suddenly illuminated a floor plan that was much the same as his own. He was standing in the sitting room surrounded by soft-cushioned cane furniture; there was an open-plan kitchen in one corner and two doors which had to lead to a bathroom and the only bedroom.

'Eve?' he called out again as he wove through the cane furniture to get to the other two doors. One was slightly ajar; warily he lifted a hand and widened the opening enough to allow light to seep into the darkened room.

What he saw brought him to a dead stand-still. The room looked like a disaster area, with Eve sitting in the middle of it like a discarded piece of the debris. Lamp light shone onto her down-bent head and her hair was all over the place, forming a tumbling screen of silk that completely hid her face. She was hugging her-self, slender arms crossed over her body, long fingers curled like talons around the back of her neck. The tattered remains of the hot-pink dress lay in a crumpled huddle beside her on the floor.

'God in heaven,' he breathed, feeling his heart drop to his stomach when he realised what had clearly been going on here.

'Go away,' she told him, the whimpered lit-tle command almost choked through a throat full with tears.

Grimly ignoring the command, Ethan walked forward, face honed into the kind of mask that would have scared the life out of Eve if she'd glanced up and seen it. He came to squat down in front of her. He might not be able to see her face but he could feel her distress pulsing out towards him.

'Are you hurt?' he asked gruffly, reaching out with a hand to lightly touch her hair.

Her response was stunning. In a single violent movement she rose to her feet, spun her back to him, then began trembling as her battle with tears began to be lost.

Ethan took his time in rising to his full height and trying to decide what his next move should be. It was as clear as day that some sort of assault had taken place here, that Eve was shocked and distressed and maybe—

'I hate you, do you know that?' she choked out suddenly. 'I really—really hate you for coming in here like this!'

'I heard a scream, came out to investigate and saw someone leaving here,' he felt compelled to explain. 'There was something in the way he moved that made me—Eve—' he changed tack anxiously '—you're shaking so badly you look like you're going to collapse. Let me—'

'Don't touch me,' she breathed, then quite suddenly her legs gave away on her and she sank, folding like a piece of limp rubber down onto the edge of the rumpled bed.

Standing there, Ethan was uncertain as to what to do next. She didn't want him near her, she wanted him to go, but there was no way he could do that without making sure she was fit to be left on her own. His eyes fell on the hot-pink dress, then the scrappy pink bra lying beside it. His skin began to crawl again in response to the horror that was painting itself into his head. The evidence suggested rape, or at the very least a bungled attempt.

A thrust of bloody anger had him bending down to scoop up a white cotton sheet from the tangle of bedding on the floor, then carefully draping the sheet around her trembling frame. It wasn't that she was naked, because he'd noticed the pair of pink panties when she'd risen to her feet. But, as for the rest... His teeth clenched together as he lowered himself into a squatting position in front of her again.

She was clutching the sheet now, face still hidden, hunched shoulders trembling like mad. 'What happened here, Eve?' he questioned grimly.

'What do you think?' she shot back on a bitter choke. 'I suppose you think I deserved it!'

'No,' he denied that.

'Liar.' She sobbed and lifted the sheet up to use it to cover her face.

'Eve—nobody of sane mind would believe a woman deserves what appears to have happened here,' he insisted soberly.

'I'm drunk,' she admitted.

He could smell the alcohol.

'It was all my fault.'

'No,' he said again, his hands hanging limp between his spread thighs, though they desperately wanted to reach out and touch her.

'I can't feel my legs. I don't even know how I got here. I think he spiked my last drink.'

'Possibly,' Ethan quietly agreed, willing to feed her answering remarks if it helped him to understand just what had happened here.

She moved at last, rubbing the sheet over her face then slowly lowering it so he could get his first look at it. Her lips were swollen and he could see chafe marks from a man's rough beard. His jaw became a solid piece of rock as he noticed other things and tried to keep that knowledge off his face.

Maybe she saw something—he wasn't sure, but she released the sheet and rubbed trembling fingers over the side of her neck, then lifted the fingers higher to push back her hair and clutched at her head as she began to rock to and fro again.

Ethan's fingers twitched; she saw it happen. 'I'm all right,' she said jerkily. 'I just need to—'

Get a hold on what has happened to me, he finished for her mentally. 'How bad was it?' He had to ask the question even though he knew she did not want to answer it. But this could well be the kind of scene that required a doctor and the police to investigate.

But Eve shook her head, refusing to answer. Then, from seemingly out of nowhere, a huge sob shook her from shoulders to feet and she was suddenly gulping out the tears with a total loss of composure.

A silent sigh ripped at the lining of his chest. 'Look, Eve, will you let me hold you? You need to be held but I don't want to—'

'You hate me.' She sobbed.

'No, I don't.' This time the sigh was full-bodied and heavy. 'I'll go and call the police.' He went to get up.

'No!' she cried, and without any warning she slid to the ground between his spread knees and landed heavily against his chest, almost knocking him over in the process.

As he flexed muscles to maintain his balance, she began sobbing brokenly into his shoulder. It was a dreadful sound—the sound nightmares were made of. Her arms went around his neck and began clinging tightly. The sheet began to slip, and with his jaw locked like a vice against the gamut of primitive emotion building inside him, Ethan caught the sheet, replaced it over her shoulders, then took a chance and wrapped his arms round her to just hold her while she cried herself out.

Her tears began to wet his shoulder and neck, mingling with her breath as she sobbed and quivered. She smelt of alcohol and something much more sweetly subtle, and he hoped she hadn't noticed that her naked breasts were pressing against his equally naked chest. She felt warm and soft and so infinitely fragile it was like holding a priceless piece of art. As his eyes took in the debacle of their surroundings, he couldn't think of a less likely setting or situation to discover that he was holding the perfect woman in his arms.

The unexpected thought stopped his train of thought. Maybe he tensed; he was certainly shocked enough to have turned into a pillar of rock. Whatever, the sobbing grew less wretched, the grip on his neck began to ease. Old tensions erupted, defensive barriers began to climb back into place. He could actually feel Eve taking stock of the situation. The sobs quietened, silence came and within it her distress changed to a self-conscious embarrassment.

She had noticed the intimacy of their embrace.

Untangling her fingers from round his neck, Eve lifted her head out of his shoulder, then drew away from him just enough to gather the sheeting around her front. She couldn't believe she had done that—couldn't believe she had just sobbed her heart out on Ethan Hayes of all people, nor that she had done it with her bare breasts flattened against his naked chest.

So now what did she do? she asked herself helplessly, and put a hand up to cover the aching throb taking place behind her heavy eyes. He didn't speak, though she wished he would because she just didn't know what to say to him.

'I'm sorry,' were the weak words that eventually left her.

'Please don't be,' he returned, sounding so stiff and formal that she wanted to shrivel up and die.

But at least he moved at last by sitting back on his ankles to place some much needed distance between them, and Eve dared herself a glance at that hair-covered chest she could still feel warm and prickly against her breasts. She liked the sensation, just as she liked the way she could taste the moist warmth of his skin on her lips.

Oh—what is happening to me? In trembling confusion brought the sheet up to cover her face again. Beyond her hiding place the silence in the room throbbed. What was he thinking?

What did he really want to do? Get up and leave? Wishing he hadn't come in here at all? Why not? She knew what Ethan Hayes thought of her. She knew he was seeing only what he would have expected to see.

In his eyes she was a flirt, a man-teaser with no scruples to stop her from going that step too far. Well, Mr Hayes, she thought behind the now damp sheet. Here I am where you probably always predicted I would end up, hoisted by my own petard.

'Say something!' she snapped out. She couldn't bear the silence.

'Tell me what happened here.'

'I don't remember!' The words and their accompanying sob drove her to her feet. Only, her legs wouldn't support her; they felt like two rubber bands stretched so taut they quivered. And how he knew that, she didn't understand! But he was on his feet and using a hand on her arm to support her as he guided her down onto the edge of the bed.

She was in shock. In one part of her wretched head, Eve was aware of that. She was even able to appreciate that Ethan did not quite know what to do in the situation he found himself in.

'I'm sorry,' she said again. 'I can't seem to th-think straight.' Taking a deep breath she made a concerted effort to be rational. 'W-we were all at Aidan's beach house. It was my birthday party and I suppose we were all a little bit tipsy. Aidan was mixing cocktails...'

Her voice trailed off, her mind drifting back over the following few minutes when Raoul had sat down beside her and they'd talked and had drunk...

After that she could remember nothing until she'd found herself back here and Raoul had been undressing her. 'It's okay, Eve.' She echoed Raoul's soothing words back to herself, unaware that what had come before had only been replayed inside her head. 'You are back home. I am putting you to bed...'

Bed. Her stomach revolted, forcing her back to her feet and off that dreadful piece of furniture! On her rubber-band legs she stumbled, her hand went out to grab at something to steady herself with and it had to be a rock-solid bicep belonging to Ethan Hayes. The worst of it was, she didn't want to let go again.

She *never* wanted to let go! Why was that? she asked herself dizzily. Why was it that this man with this cold hard expression that so disapproved of her, could fill her with such a warm feeling of strength of trust?

She didn't know. In fact she didn't think she knew anything for certain any more. 'I believed him.' Staring up at Ethan's mask-like face, her own revealed a shocked lack of comprehension at her own gullibility. 'How could I have *done* that?' she cried. 'How could I *not* have known there was more to his motives than…?'

'He spiked your drink,' Ethan gently reminded her. 'Don't knock yourself over something I don't believe you had any control over.'

Swallowing she nodded and clutched more tightly at his arm. 'I m-must have passed out again,' she went on shakily. 'Next thing I remember, I was being kissed. I thought it was a dream…' She stopped to swallow thickly, put trembling fingers up to her swollen lips and her expression crumpled on a wave of pained and frightened dismay because it had been no dream. 'I th-think I screamed. I th-think I hit

him. I think I m-managed to scramble off the
bed. I *know* I screamed again because I can
still hear it shrilling inside my h-head—'

The stumbling words were halted by the
way Ethan wrapped her close to him again. It
was the sweetest, most comforting gift he
could have given her right then.

But Ethan wasn't thinking of gifts, he was
thinking of murder. He was seeing Aidan
Galloway's handsome face and how it was going to look when he had restructured it. He was
thinking about how this proud, feisty woman
had been reduced to this, because one spoiled
lout didn't know how to control his libido. He
was also thinking about the way she came into
his arms without hesitation, how she was nestling here.

'I thought he was my friend.'

Ethan recognised the pained feeling that
went into that wretched comment. 'We all
make poor judgements of people now and
then.'

She nodded against his breastbone—he
wished she wouldn't do that he thought, as
other parts of him began to respond. He
wished he understood it, wished he knew why

this woman had the power to move him in ways he'd never previously known. It wasn't just the sex thing, he made that clear to himself. But he liked the way she clung to him, and how, despite the ordeal she had just been through here, she could trust him enough to cling.

'You're being too nice to me.'

'You would prefer it if I tore into you about the dangers of flirting with one too many young and sexually healthy men?'

'Like you just did, you mean?' Lifting her head she looked at him through eyes turned almost black by fright and whatever drug was swimming in her blood.

Vulnerable, he thought. Too—too vulnerable. It made him want to kiss away her fears— What he didn't expect was for Eve to suddenly fall on his neck and start kissing him!

Shock leapt upon him like a scalded cat with its claws unsheathed. Those claws raked a pleasurable passage across his senses before he found the wits to prize his mouth free from hers. He had to use tough hands on her waist to prize the rest of her away from him. 'What the *hell*?' he ground out forcefully as she stood

staring up at him through those wide black un-
seeing eyes. By now he was feeling so damn
shaken he was almost on the point of running
himself! 'Dear God, Eve, what do you think
you're playing at?'

The rough-cut rake of his voice brought her
blinking back from wherever she had gone off
to. She stared at him in horror then in dawning
dismay. 'Oh,' she gasped out in a shaken
whimper, and then it was she who tried to
make a mortified bolt for it. But the moment
she tried her legs gave away once more.

On a muttered curse Ethan caught her up,
then dumped her unceremoniously back onto
the bed. The whole thing was taking on a sur-
real quality. Standing there he stared down at
her as if she was some kind of alien while she
rocked and groaned with a hand flattened
across her horrified mouth. It was then as he
watched her that it really began to dawn on
him that the swine must have spiked her drink
with something pretty potent and it was still
very much at work in her blood. 'I'm sorry,'
she was saying over and over. 'I don't know
what came over me. I don't—'

'You need a doctor,' Ethan decided grimly.

'No!'

'We need to call in the police and get them to track that bastard down so that we can find out what it is he's slipped you.'

'No,' she groaned out a second time.

But Ethan wasn't listening. He was too busy looking around for the telephone. As Eve saw him take a stride towards one sitting on a low table across the room, she erupted with a panic that flung her anxiously to her feet.

'No, Ethan—please—!' she begged him. 'No police. No doctor—I'm all right!'

Virtually staggering in her quest to put herself between him and the phone, she stood there trembling and looking pleadingly up at him while he looked down at her with an expression that grimly mocked her assurance.

'I *will* be all right in a minute or two!' she temporised, saw him take another determined step and felt the tears begin to burn in her eyes as fresh anxiety swelled like a monster inside. 'Please—' she begged again. 'You don't understand. The scandal, my grandfather—he will blame himself and I couldn't *bear* to let him do that!' I can't bear to know that he will never look on me in the same way again, Eve added in silent anguish. 'Look...' at least Ethan was no longer moving, and the panic had placed the strength back in her legs '...I was drunk. It was my own f-fault—'

'There is no excuse out there to justify date rape, Eve,' Ethan toughly contested.

'B-but it didn't get that far. I m-managed to stop him before he could—' The words dried up. She just couldn't bring herself to say them and had to swallow on a lump of nausea instead. 'I'll get over this—I will!' she insisted. 'But *only* if we can keep it a secret between you and me; please, Ethan—please—!' she repeated painfully.

She was pleading with him as if she was pleading for her life here, but Ethan could see the lingering horror in her eyes, see the shock and hurt and bewildered sense of betrayal, see the swollen mouth and the chafed skin, and the effects of some nasty substance that had turned her beautiful eyes black and had left her barely able to control her actions.

Did she really expect him to simply ignore all of that? In an act of frustrating indecision he sent his eyes lashing around the room. It looked like exactly what it was: the scene of some vile crime. The man was dangerous; he needed to be stopped and made to pay for his actions.

Flicking his gaze back to Eve, Ethan opened his mouth to tell her just that—then stopped, the breath stilling in his lungs when he saw the tears in her eyes, the trembling mouth, the anxiety in her pale face that was now overshadowing the incident itself. His mouth snapped shut. A sigh rattled from him. Surrender to her pleas arrived when he acknowledged that she was in no fit state to take any more tonight.

'Okay,' he agreed with grim reluctance. 'We will leave the rest until tomorrow. But for now you can't stay here on your own...'

He deliberately didn't add, '...in case he comes back'. But he saw by her shuddering response that Eve had added the words for herself. 'Thank you,' she whispered.

He didn't want thanks. He wanted a solution as to what he was going to do next. Glancing at Eve in search of inspiration, he found himself looking at a wilting flower again, only she was a slender white lily this time, covered as she was in the cotton sheet.

A sad and helpless slender white lily, he
elaborated, and the image locked up a blistering kind of anger inside his chest. 'How are
you feeling?' he asked gruffly. 'Do you think
you can manage to get yourself dressed?'

'Yes,' she whispered.

'Good.' He nodded. At least she was managing to stand unsupported at last. 'Do that,
then I'll walk you up to the main house,' he
decided, aware that there was a small army of
live-in staff up there to watch over her.

'No, not the house.' Once again she vetoed
his suggestion. 'The staff will report to my
grandfather and…' Her voice trailed away, and
those big eyes were suddenly pleading with
him again. 'Could I come and stay with you?'
she asked. 'Just for the rest of tonight. I promise I won't be any more trouble, only…'

Again that voice trailed away to nothing,
and that dark, sad, vulnerable look cut into him
with a deeply painful thrust. Hell, how was it
he seemed to attract these kind of situations?
he wondered, racking his brain for an alternative solution only to find there wasn't one.
Beginning to feel a bit as if he'd been run over

by a bus, he lifted up a hand in a hopeless gesture. 'Sure,' he said.

Why not? he asked himself fatalistically. He had conceded to just about everything else.

He was just about to leave her to it when he saw her mouth open to offer yet another pathetic thanks. 'Don't say it,' he advised grimly.

'No,' she mumbled understandingly. 'Sorry,' she offered instead.

His shoulder muscles rippled as they flexed in irritation. 'Don't say that either,' he clipped out tightly. 'I don't want your thanks or your apologies.' What he really wanted, he thought as he turned for the bedroom door, was to close his hands around Aidan Galloway's throat.

He was angry, Eve realised. She didn't blame him. She had probably managed to thoroughly ruin his holiday with all of this. Feeling sick to her stomach, as weak as a kitten, and still too shocked and dizzy to really comprehend even half of what had happened to her tonight, she turned away from him with the weary intention of doing as she'd been told and finding some clothes to put on—only to go still on a strangled gasp when she found herself confronted with her own reflection in the mirror on the opposite wall.

The sound brought Ethan's departure to a halt. Glancing back, he followed her gaze, found himself looking at her reflection in the mirror and instantly understood.

She'd seen her swollen mouth, her chafed skin—had caught sight of the telling discolouration on the side of her neck that Ethan had been trying very hard to ignore from the moment he'd seen it himself. And perhaps most telling of all was the pink hibiscus still trying its best to cling to her hair.

The tears bulged in her eyes. 'I look like a harlot,' she whispered tremulously, lifting shaking fingers to remove the poor flower.

A sensationally beautiful, very special harlot, he silently extended, and on that provoking thought he threw in the metaphorical towel. 'Blow the clothes,' he decided harshly and walked back to her side. His arm came to rest across her sheet swathed shoulders. 'Let's just get you out of here.'

With that he grimly urged her into movement. Still shocked at the sight of herself, Eve tripped over the trailing sheet. On a muttered curse, Ethan went the whole hog and scooped her up high against his chest.

'I can walk!' she protested.

'Enjoy the ride,' was his curt response, as he began carrying her out of the bedroom and out of the house with his cast-iron expression brooking no argument.

Neither saw the dark figure standing in the shadows, whose eyes followed their journey from one beach house to the other by the conventional route of paths and gates. Eve's attention was just too occupied with that old fascination, which was this man called Ethan Hayes and the structure of his—she was thinking, handsome, but the word was really too soft to describe such a forcefully masculine face. His chin was square and slightly chiselled, his eyelashes long and thick. His eyebrows were two sternly straight black bars that dipped a little towards the bridge of his nose and added a disturbing severity she rather liked. She liked his eyes too, even with that a dark steely glint they were reflecting right now, and she loved his mouth, its size, its shape, its smooth firm texture— Her lips began to pulse with the sudden dark urge to taste him in that same wild, uncontrolled way she had done a few minutes ago.

Had she really done that? Shock ricocheted through her. *Why* had she done it? What kind of substance could Raoul have stirred into her drink that had had the power to make her do such an outrageous thing? She shifted uncomfortably, disturbed by the knowledge that such an out-of-control person could actually be lurking inside her, seemingly waiting the chance to leap out and jump all over a man. What must he be thinking about it, and her, and—?

'About that kiss earlier...' she said, approaching the subject tentatively.

Long eyelashes flickered, steely grey irises glinting as he glanced down at her upturned face. 'Forget it,' he advised, and looked away again because Ethan was trying not to think at all.

It was hard enough trying not to be aware that what he was carrying was feather-light and as slender as a reed, and that the warm body beneath the sheet was shapely and sleek. He didn't need the added provocation of looking into her beautiful face, nor to be reminded of that unexpected kiss.

So he concentrated his mind on the different ways he could make Aidan Galloway sorry for what he had done to Eve tonight. Date rape— for want of something to call it—and the use of sexually enhancing drugs to get what he desired, made Galloway the lowest form of human life.

That was where Eve's kiss had come from, he reminded himself. Nothing more, nothing less, therefore not worth a second thought.

So why can you still feel the imprint of her mouth against your own? he asked himself grimly.

Because she was beautiful, because she was dangerous, and—heaven help him—he liked the danger Eve Herakleides represented. It was called sexual attraction, and he would have to be a fool not to be aware that Eve felt the same pull. That little wriggle she'd just performed had been full of sexual tension—though he had to concede that the drink probably had had a lot to do with it too.

Either way, it was a danger he could not afford to be tempted by. His life was complicated enough without the tempting form of Eve Herakleides.

So what do you think you are doing now? he then scoffed to himself as he carried Eve in through his own front door. And discovered it was not a question he wanted to answer right now, as he lowered her feet to the floor then turned to close the door.

CHAPTER FIVE

THE beach houses were all very picturesque outside, but very basic inside; just one bedroom, a bathroom, small kitchen and a sitting room. Really they were meant for nothing more than a place to cool off during a day spent on the beach. Or as in Ethan case, the perfect place for the single person to use for a holiday. Problems only arose when the single person doubled to two.

It was a problem that only began to dawn on Eve as she watched Ethan close the door. The fact that it had dawned on him too at about the same moment became apparent when, instead of turning to face her, he went perfectly still.

A thick and uncomfortable silence settled between them. Clutching the sheet to her throat, Eve tried to think of something to say to break through the awkward atmosphere. Ethan tried to break it by taking off round the room to switch on the table lamps.

The light hurt her eyes, forcing her to squeeze them shut. He noticed. 'Sorry,' he murmured. 'I didn't think—'

'It's okay.' She made herself open them again. She didn't look at him though—she couldn't. Instead she made a play of checking out her surroundings—surroundings she already knew as well as she knew her own, because she had been in and out of the Petronades beach house since early childhood.

'Bedroom through that door, bathroom the other...'

She looked and nodded. Her mouth felt paper dry.

'Would you like a drink? Something hot like tea or coffee?'

Yes—no, Eve thought in tense confusion. Her head was beginning to pound, a sense of disorientation washing over her in ever increasing waves. She felt strange, out of place and—

'This was a mistake,' she pushed out thickly. 'I think I had better—'

One small step in the direction of the front door was all that it took for the whole wretched nightmare to come crashing back down upon her head. She swayed dizzily, felt her legs turn back to rubber; she knew she was going to do something stupid like drop to the floor in a tent of white sheeting.

Only it never happened, because he was already at her side and catching hold of her arms to steady her. She was trembling so badly her teeth actually chattered.

'Are you frightened of being alone here with me, or is this a delayed shock reaction?' he questioned soberly.

Both, Eve thought. 'Sh-shock, I think,' was the answer she gave out loud. Then she confessed to him shakily, 'Ethan, I really need to sit down.'

'What you need is a doctor,' he clipped back tautly.

'No,' she refused.

Sighing at her stubbornness. 'Bed, then,' he insisted. 'You can at least sleep off the effects there.'

He was about to lift her back into his arms when Eve stopped him. 'W-what I would really love to do is take a shower,' she told him. 'W-wash his touch from my skin...'

There was another one of those tense pauses. 'Eve, he didn't—?'

'No,' she put in quickly. 'He didn't.' But the tremors became shudders, and neither of them bothered to question why she was suddenly shuddering so badly.

'The bathroom it is, then,' he said briskly, and the next thing she knew Eve was being lifted into his arms again and carried into the bathroom. He set her down on the lowered toilet seat, then turned to switch on the shower. 'Stay right there,' he instructed then as he was disappearing through the door.

His departure gave Eve the opportunity to sag weakly. He was back in seconds, though, forcing her to straighten her backbone before he caught her looking so darn pathetic.

'Fresh towels,' he announced, settling them on the washbasin. 'And a tee shirt of mine.' He placed it on her lap. 'I thought it might be more comfortable to wear than the sheet.'

It was an attempt to lighten the thick atmosphere with humour, Eve recognised, and did her best to rise to it. 'White was never my colour,' she murmured, referring to the sheet.

The tee shirt was white. They both stared down at it. It was such a stupid, mild, incidental little error that certainly did not warrant the flood of hot tears it produced. Ethan saw them—of course he did—when had he missed a single thing since he'd barged into her bedroom?

He came to squat down in front of her. 'Hey,' he murmured gently. 'It's okay. I am not offended that you don't like my tee shirt.'

But she did like it. She liked every single thing about this man, every single thing he had done for her. And the worst of it was that he had done it all even though he actively disliked her! 'I'm so very sorry for dumping on you like this.' The sheet was covering her face again.

'I thought we'd agreed that you were not going to apologise,' he reminded her.

'But I feel so wretched, and I know you have to be hating this.'

'I hate what happened to you to put us both in this situation,' he tempered. 'And the rest I think is best left until tomorrow when you should be feeling more able to cope.'

He was right. Eve nodded. 'I'll take that shower now,' she said bracingly.

'You will be okay on your own? You won't fall over or—?'

'I'll be okay.' She nodded.

He didn't look too sure about that. His eyebrows were touching across the bridge of his nose as he studied her, and his eyes were no longer steely but dark and deep with genuine worry and concern. Could she *ever* look more pathetic than this? Eve wondered tragically. And did it *have* to be Ethan Hayes who witnessed it?

The sheet was used as a handkerchief again, and they weren't her fingers that lifted it to wipe the tears from her cheeks, they were his gentle fingers. The caring act was almost her complete undoing.

'I'll be fine!' she promised in near desperation. Any second now she was going to throw herself at him again if she didn't get him out of here! 'Please go, Ethan—please,' she repeated plaintively.

Maybe he knew because he rose up to his full height. 'Don't lock the door,' was his final comment. 'And if you need me, shout.'

But Eve didn't shout, and while he waited for her to reappear, Ethan prowled the place. He was like a pacing tiger guarding his territory—he likened his own tense and restless state. In the end he put his restless energy to use and tidied the bedroom, remade the bed and, as a belated thought, pulled another clean tee shirt out of the drawer and slid it over his head, then went to make a pot of tea. He had just been placing a tray down on the coffee table when the bathroom door opened.

He glanced up. Eve paused in the doorway. She had a towel wrapped around her hair and she was wearing the tee shirt. It covered her to halfway down her thighs and the short sleeves almost brushed her slender wrists.

She was wrong about the colour, he thought, quickly dropping his eyes away. 'Tea?' he offered.

'I... Yes, please,' she answered and, after a small hesitation that told him Eve was as uncomfortable with this situation as he was, she walked forward and took the chair next to the sofa. Having been told how she liked her tea, Ethan poured and offered her the mug then folded himself into the other chair. Neither spoke as they sipped, and the atmosphere was strained, to put it mildly. Eve was the first to attempt to ease it. Putting the cup down on the tray, she removed the towel from her hair and shook out its wet and tangled length. 'Would you have a comb or something I could use?'

'Sure.' Glad of the excuse to move, he got up and found a comb. 'Hair-dryer's in the bathroom,' he said as he handed over the comb.

She nodded in acknowledgement of something he suspected she already knew. He sat down again and she began combing the tangles out of her hair. It was all very domestic, very we-do-this-kind-of-thing-all-the-time.   But nothing could have been further from the truth.

'I'll take the couch,' she said.

'No, you won't,' he countered. 'I have my honour to protect. *I* take the couch.'

'But—'

'Not up for discussion,' he cut in on her protest. One brief glance at his face and she was conceding the battle to him. Suddenly she looked utterly exhausted yet so uptight that the grip she had on his comb revealed shiny white knuckles.

'Come on, you've had enough.' Standing up again, he swung himself into action which felt better than sitting there feeling useless. Taking hold of her wrist, he tugged her to her feet, gently prized the comb from her fingers, and began trailing her towards the bedroom.

'My hair...' she prompted.

'It won't fall out if you leave it to dry by itself,' was his sardonic answer. But really he knew he was rushing her like this because it was himself that had suddenly had enough. He needed some space that didn't have Eve Herakleides in it. He needed to get a hold on what was churning up his insides.

And what was that? he asked himself. He refused to let himself look for the answer because he knew it was likely to make him as bad as that swine Aidan Galloway.

The bedroom was ready and waiting, its shadows softened by the gentle glow from the bedside lamp. He saw Eve glance at the bed, then at the room as a whole, and her nervous uncertainty almost screamed in this latest silence to develop between them.

'You're safe here, Eve,' he grimly assured her, making that assurance on the back of his own sinful thoughts.

She nodded, slipped her wrist out of his grasp and took a couple of steps away. She looked so darn lost and anxious that he had to wonder if she was picking up on what his own tension was about.

Yet what did she do next? She floored him by suddenly spinning to face him. White-faced, big-eyed, small mouth trembling. 'Will you stay?' she burst out. 'Just for a few minutes. I don't want to be alone yet. I...'

The moment she'd said it, Eve was wishing the stupid words back. Just the expression on his face was enough to tell her she could not have appalled him more if she'd tried. Oh, damn, she thought and put a trembling hand up to cover her face. He didn't even like her; hadn't she always known that? Yet here she was almost begging him to sleep with her—or as good as.

'Pretend I never said that,' she retracted, turned away and even managed a couple more steps towards the wretched bed! She felt dizzy and confused and terribly disorientated—and she wished Raoul Delacroix had never been born!

The arm that reached round her to flip back the bed covers almost startled her out of her wits. 'In,' Ethan commanded.

In, like a child being put to bed by a stern father, she likened. *In* she got, curling onto her side like a child and let him settle the covers over her. When I leave here tomorrow I am *never* going to let myself set eyes on Ethan Hayes again! she vowed. 'Goodnight,' she made herself say.

'Shut up,' he returned and the next thing she knew he was stretching out beside her on top of the covers. 'I'll stay until you go to sleep,' he announced.

'You don't have to,' Eve responded with a hint of bite. 'I changed my mind. I don't—' The way he turned on his side to face her was enough to push the rest of her words back down her throat.

'Now listen to me, you aggravating little witch,' he said huskily. 'Any more provocation from you and I am likely to lose my temper. If you need me here, I'll stay, if you want me to go, I'll go. Your decision.'

Her decision. 'Stay,' she whispered.

Without another word he flopped onto his back and stared rigidly at the ceiling. Curled up at his side, Eve imagined his silent curses that were probably all very colourful ways of describing what he was feeling about this mess.

I'm sorry, she wanted to say, but she knew he didn't want to hear that, so she did the next best thing she could think of and shut her eyes then willed herself to fall asleep.

Five minutes, Ethan was thinking grimly. I'll give her five minutes to fall asleep then I'm out of here. With that, he took a look at his watch. Two o'clock.

A sigh whispered from her. Turning his head it wrenched at his heart to see the trace of tears still staining her cheeks. She had just endured a close encounter with what had to be a woman's worst nightmare and here he was putting a time limit on how long he was going to support her through the rest of this.

A sigh whispered from him. Eve liked the sigh. She liked the comfort she gained from hearing his closeness and the sure knowledge that if she was safe anywhere then it had to be right here with him.

Tomorrow was destined to be another thing entirely. By tomorrow, she predicted, it would be back to hostilities, with him backing off whenever she threatened to come close. But, for now, she was content to think of him as her guardian angel, and on that comforting thought she let herself relax into sleep.

Another five minutes, Ethan decided. She'd relaxed at last and her breathing was steady. He would give her another five minutes to slip into a deep slumber, then he would swap the comfort of the bed for the discomfort of the living-room couch.

His eyelids began to droop; he dragged them back up again and captured a yawn on the back of his hand. Eve moved and mumbled something, it sounded like, 'Don't.' He tagged on another five minutes because the last thing he wanted was for her to wake up in a strange bed alone and frightened. Another five minutes wouldn't kill him, would it?

Eve came thrashing up from a deep dark sleep to that halfway place where haunted dream mixed with confusing reality. A sound had disturbed her, though she wasn't sure what it had represented, only that it had made her pulse accelerate and had pushed up her eyelids so she found herself staring directly into the sleeping face of Ethan Hayes. He was lying kiss-close to her on the same pillow with his arms and legs wrapped warmly around her— or were her limbs wrapped around him? She didn't have time to consider the puzzle because the sound came again and even as she lifted her head off the pillow she was aware that Ethan was now awake also. They turned together to look towards the open bedroom doorway, then froze on a heart-stopping clutch of stunning dismay.

Theron Herakleides stood filling the doorway, looking like his favourite god, Zeus, with his thickly curling grey locks framing a rough, tough, lived-in face that was clearly preparing to cast thunderbolts down on their heads.

'Grandpa,' Eve only managed on a strangled whisper. Ethan hissed out a couple of quick curses beneath his breath. The old man flicked devil-to-pay black eyes from one to the other and conjured up an image of themselves, which showed them what he was seeing. It was so utterly damning neither found the ability to speak in their own defence.

Theron did it for them when hard as rock, he threw his first thunderbolt. 'One hour, in my study at the main house,' he instructed. 'I will expect you both there.'

Then he was gone, leaving them lying there in a tangle of limbs and white bedding, feeling as culpable as a pair of guilty lovers who'd been caught red-handed in the act of sex.

'Oh, dear God.' Eve found her voice first, groaning out the words as she fell back heavily against the bed.

Ethan went one stage further and snaked his legs free of the tangle then landed on his feet beside the bed. He did not want to believe that any of this was really happening.

'How did you get here?' Eve had the absolute stupidity to ask him.

'How did *I* get here?' Ethan swung round to lance at her. 'This is *my* bed!'

They'd both reacted on pure instinct. Now reality hit, clearing away the last muddy remnants of sleep. Eve began to remember. Ethan watched it happen in a slide-frame flicker, as she passed through last night's ordeal to this morning's shocked horror. She went as pale as alabaster, clamped a hand across her trembling mouth, and just stared at him through huge dark nightmare-ridden eyes that turned his insides into a raging inferno of anger and gave him a desire to break someone's neck.

His own at the moment, he acknowledged grimly, and released the air from his lungs on a pressured hiss. 'My fault,' he conceded. 'I fell asleep. I'll go and talk to him.'

Decision set in his mind, he was already turning towards the door when Eve's half hysterical, 'No!' hit his ears. 'He won't believe you. I have to do it!' She began scrambling shakily to the edge of the bed. All long limbs, flying hair and utterly shattered composure, she landed on her feet beside him and began searching the floor.

'Shoes,' she mumbled anxiously.

'You didn't come in shoes. I carried you, remember?'

The hand was at her mouth again as a second barrage of memories came flooding in. No shoes, no clothes; Ethan was seeing it all with her. He was also seeing another bed that had looked not unlike this one, with its covers lying in the same damning tangle, half on the floor half on the bed.

Had Theron Herakleides seen that other bed too? His skin began to prickle as he began to fully appreciate what the older man had to believe from the evidence. A passionate interlude spent in his granddaughter's bed before they'd transferred to this one to repeat the whole orgy all over again.

The air left his lungs on yet another hard hiss. This whole mad scenario was going to take some serious explaining. 'I'll do the explaining,' he grimly insisted. 'You can stay here while I—'

'Will you listen to me, Ethan—? He will not believe you!' Eve stated fiercely. 'Trust me. I know him. He has seen what he's seen.'

'The truth is out there, Eve,' he reminded her. 'It has a name and a face—and when I get my hands on him he will be happy to spill out the truth to your grandfather.'

While his eyes began to darken at the delightful prospect of bringing Aidan Galloway face to face with his sins, Eve's eyes did the opposite and turned bright green, glinting like the eyes of a witch who was busy concocting her next wicked spell. She started walking towards the door.

'Where are you going?' he demanded.

'To see Grandpa before you do,' she stated firmly.

'Eve—'

'No!' She turned on him. 'I said I will deal with it!' The eyes were now glinting with tears, not wicked spells. 'Y-you don't understand. You will *never* understand!' And on that she was gone, running out of the room and leaving him standing there wondering what the heck that last outburst had been all about?

He'd understood! Of course he'd understood, he claimed arrogantly. From the moment he'd stepped into her bedroom last night, he'd understood without question what it was he'd been seeing!

Now it hurt that *she* didn't see that understanding. What did she think he was going to do? Paint her character all the lurid colours he could think of just to make his own part in this fiasco seem prettier?

Well, he was damned if he was going to slink away and hide in some dark corner while Eve fought his battles for him. Theron Herakleides was expecting the two of them to present themselves in his study and that was what would happen.

CHAPTER SIX

UNDERSTANDING anything about Eve Herakleides flew out of the window the moment Ethan found himself confronting her grandfather. Because Eve, he all too quickly discovered, had got in first with her version of events leading up to what Theron had witnessed. Now Ethan was angrily trying to make some sense of what it was he was supposed to have done.

Standing tall and proud behind his desk, Theron Herakleides looked on Ethan as if he was seeing a snake in the grass. 'You have to appreciate, Mr Hayes,' he was saying, 'that in Greece we expect a man to stand by his actions.'

'Are you implying that I wouldn't?' Ethan demanded stiffly.

The older man's brief smile set his temper simmering. 'You stand here claiming no intimacy between yourself and my granddaughter,' he pointed out. 'Are those not the words

93

of a man who is trying to wriggle off the hook he finds himself caught upon?'

'We were not intimate,' Ethan insisted angrily.

A pair of grey-cloud eyebrows rose enquiringly. 'Now you expect this old man to question what his own eyes have already told him?'

Not only his own eyes, Ethan noted, as he sent a murderous glance at Eve who was standing quietly beside her grandfather. Gone was the seductress in sexy hot-pink. Nor was there any sign of the broken little creature he'd taken under his wing. No, from the neatly braided hair to the clothes that had been chosen with modesty in mind, here stood a picture of sweet innocence wearing a butter-wouldn't-melt-in-her-mouth smile that told clearly that he was going to be made the scapegoat here!

'Of course,' Theron Herakleides broke into speech again, 'you could be attempting to protect Eve's reputation, in which case I most sincerely apologise for implying the opposite. But your protection comes too late, I'm afraid,' he informed him gravely. 'For what I saw with my own eyes had already been substantiated by one of the men that guard my property. He saw you carry my granddaughter from our beach house to your beach house covered only by a sheet, you see...'

Damned by his own actions, Ethan realised. Then he said frowningly, 'Just a minute. If your guard was watching the beach house, then where was he when Eve—?'

Eve moved, drawing his glance and lodging the rest of his challenge in his throat when he found those eyes of hers pleading with him to say no more. Anger erupted as he glared at her and felt frustration mount like a boiling lump of matter deep within his chest.

I should stop this right here, he told himself forcefully. I should tell Eve's grandfather the unvarnished truth and finish this craziness once and for all. But those pleading eyes were pricking anxiously at him, reminding him of the conversation he and Eve had had the night before.

Ethan looked back at her grandfather, and Eve held her breath. If he talked, it was over. If he talked, her life was never going to be the same again.

'I think it's time you explained to me where you are going with this, Theron,' Ethan invited very grimly.

A deep sense of relief relaxed the tension out of Eve's shoulders. Thank you, she wanted to say to him. Thank you from the bottom of my heart for this.

'I am going to give you the benefit of the doubt,' her grandfather smoothly announced, 'and presume that your intentions towards my granddaughter are entirely honourable...'

It wasn't a question but a rock-solid statement. Eve watched nervously as Ethan's full attention became riveted on the older man's face. Her heart stopped beating in the throbbing silence, her mouth running dry, as she tried to decide whether to jump in and take over before Ethan said something ruinous or to remain quiet and keep praying that he didn't let her down.

Ethan didn't know what he was doing. The word 'honourable' was playing over and over inside his head while he stared at Theron's perfectly blank expression. Then he switched his gaze to Eve who was standing there looking like a diehard romantic who'd just had her dearest wish voiced out loud.

I've been well and truly set up, he finally registered, and the knowledge was threatening to cut him off at the knees.

Eve came to his rescue—if it could be called a rescue. Leaving her grandfather's side she rounded the desk and came to thread her fingers in with his then had the gall to lean lovingly against him like an ecstatic bride. 'You guessed our secret.' She pouted at her darling grandpa. 'I'm so happy! This is turning out to be the most wonderful birthday of my entire life.'

Slowly turning his dark head Ethan looked down at her through narrowed, steely I'm-going-kill-you eyes. 'Oh, don't be cross.' She pouted at him also. 'I know you wanted to wait a while before we told anyone about us. But Grandpa can keep a secret—can't you, Grandpa?' It was Grandpa's turn to receive the full spell-casting blast of her wide green witch's eyes.

The old man smiled. It was an action that smoothed every hard angle out of him. 'But why be secretive, my little angel?' he quizzed fondly. 'You are in love with each other. Don't hide it, celebrate! We will announce your betrothal in front of the family when we return to Athens next week...'

*   *   *

He's remembered he hates me, Eve realised nervously. Ethan had washed and changed before coming up to the main house, but even wearing a smart blue shirt and grey trousers she could still see the man sitting in the beach bar feeding her his utter contempt.

'Please, Ethan,' she said, panting as she hurried after him down the path that led the way back to the beach. 'Let me explain—'

'You set me up,' he rasped. 'That doesn't need explaining.'

'It was the only way I could think of to—'

'Get a marriage proposal?' he cut in contemptuously.

'You're not that good a catch!' she retaliated.

He stopped striding and swung round to face her. Sensational, Eve thought with an inner flutter. Ethan Hayes in the throws of a blistering fury was exciting and dangerous and—

'Then, *why* me?' he bit out.

'He dotes on me...'

Ethan responded to that with a hard laugh. 'Now tell me something I haven't worked out.'

'He's built this shining glass case around me that he likes to believe protects me from the realities of life.'

'Take my advice, and smash the case,' Ethan responded. 'Before someone else comes along and smashes it for you.' On that he turned and started walking again.

So did Eve. 'That's the whole point,' she said urgently. 'I know I need to smash the case, but gently, Ethan!' she pleaded with him. 'Not with a cold hard blow of just about the ugliest truth I could possibly think of to hurt him with.'

'He deserves the truth,' he insisted. 'You are insulting him by protecting him from it!'

'No.' Her hand gripping his arm pulled him to a stop again, like a miniature tyrant she stepped right in front of him to block his path. Her eyes pleaded, her mouth pleaded, the fierce grasp of her fingers pleaded. 'You don't understand. He's—'

Eve watched him go from sizzling fury to another place entirely. His shoulders flexed, his teeth gritted together, his wide breastbone shifted on an excess of suppressed air. 'Don't tell me again that I don't understand,' he bit out roughly, 'when all I need to understand is that you are using me, Miss Herakleides. And that sticks right here.' He stabbed two long fingers at his throat.

'Yes, I can see that...' she nodded '...and I'm sorry...'

'Good. Now let me pass so I can go and do what I need to do.'

'Which is what?' she asked warily.

The morning sun dappling through the tree tops suddenly turned his face into a map of hard angles that made her insides start to shake. 'Find the cause of this mess and make him wish he'd never been born before I deliver him into the hands of your grandfather,' Ethan answered grittily and went to step around her.

'You can't!' Once again Eve stopped him. 'H-he isn't here!' she exclaimed. 'H-he left the island by launch at first light. I know because I checked before I went to see Grandpa. H-he must have known I—'

'You checked,' Ethan repeated, his eyes narrowing on her pale features and her worriedly stammering lips. 'Now, why should you want to go and do that?' he questioned silkily.

'I w-wanted to talk to him, f-find out why he did it,' she explained. 'I really needed to know if I had brought it all upon myself!

H-he was a friend—a long-standing friend. Friends don't do that to each other, do they? So I had to at least try to find out why!'

Ethan really couldn't believe he was hearing this. 'After everything he put you through last night.' Grimly he stuck to the main issue here. 'You went to confront him—on your own?'

Anxiety was darkening those big green eyes again. 'If I'd asked you to come with me, I knew you would want to kill him!'

Time to stop looking in those eyes, he decided. 'And you don't want him dead,' he persisted.

'No,' she breathed. 'I'm trying to avoid trouble not stir it up! A war will erupt between the two families if what happened last night ever got out.'

But that wasn't the real reason, Ethan thought grimly. She was hiding something, he was sure of it.

Then that something was suddenly clawing its way up his spine and attacking the hairs at the back of his neck. It was written all over her, in those big green apprehensive eyes, in the unsteady tremor of her lovely mouth—in the very words she had said!

ALAMEDA FREE LIBRARY

'You're in love with the bastard.' He made the outright accusation. No wonder she'd felt compelled to find out why he had done what he had done! Why she didn't want Ethan to go anywhere near him—why she was trying to protect the swine now!

Her chin shot up. 'I'm what?' she questioned in shrill surprise.

But Ethan was no longer listening. 'I can't believe what a fool I've been,' he muttered. For him it was like lightning striking twice! First, he had got embroiled in Leona's love problems. Now he found himself embroiled in Eve's!

. 'How dare you?' she gasped out, dropping the surprise for indignant fury.

'No.' Ethan hit back by turning on her furiously. 'How dare *you* get me mixed up in your crazy love life?'

He was angry; she was angry; the old hostile sparks began to fly. The air crackled with them, 'That's rich,' Eve mocked, 'coming from a man who is only here on this island because he's in hiding after being caught red-handed with another man's wife!'

The sparks changed into a high-voltage current. It was unstable—very unstable. 'Who told you that?' Ethan demanded.

Eve shrugged. 'Leandros Petronades is a relative of Grandpa's. He told Grandpa, and Grandpa thought I should know before I committed myself to you.'

'It's a lie,' he declared.

Eve didn't believe him. 'Don't insult my intelligence,' she denounced. 'Do you think I didn't notice the bruise on your face when you arrived on the island? Everyone noticed it. In fact it was the source of much speculation.'

'And the bruise on your neck?' Ethan went in with the metaphorical knife and took some satisfaction from seeing her snap her hand up to cover the mark.

'I forgot!' she gasped out in impressive horror.

Ethan didn't believe her. The brazen hussy hadn't even bothered to cover the damn thing up! 'How many more people have seen it and been equally imaginative about how it was put there?'

She blushed and looked uncomfortable. Ethan released a harsh laugh. 'My God,' he

breathed, 'you are unbelievable! Take my advice, Eve,' he offered as his grim farewell. 'Go
back up to the house and tell your grandfather
the truth before I do it for you.'

'You wouldn't...'

He was turning away when she said that. It
brought him swinging back again. 'I would,'
he promised. 'And you know why I would do
it? Because you are a danger to yourself,' he
told her. 'You flirt with every man you come
into contact with, uncaring what your flirting
is doing to them. Then you have the rank stupidity to fall in love with a piece of low life
like Aidan Galloway— And even after what
he tried to do to you last night, you are *still*
standing here protecting him! That makes you
dangerous,' he concluded, and tried to ignore
her greyish pallor, the hint of tears, the small
shocked jerk she made that somehow cut him
so deeply he almost groaned out loud.

Instead he walked away, striding down the
path towards the beach with so much anger
burning inside him he had to reign in on just
about every emotion he possessed, or he'd be
doing something really stupid like—

Like going back up the path and taking back every rotten, slaying word he'd spoken, because he knew what it was like to be in love with the wrong person, didn't he?

At least Leona was warm and kind and unfailingly loyal to her husband, he grimly justified his reason for not turning back. Aidan Galloway was a different kind of meat entirely. He was poison; he needed exposing before he tried the same thing with some other woman.

From a window in the main house, Theron Herakleides observed the altercation on the path down to the beach through mildly satisfied eyes. He wasn't quite sure what the altercation was actually about, but he had a shrewd idea. Ethan Hayes had just been well and truly scuppered by his enterprising granddaughter and he was now in the middle of a black fury.

Served him right for seducing her, Theron thought coldly. If he hadn't been so sure that Eve truly believed she was in love with the rake, the hell being wrought down there on his path would have been happening right here at his own orchestration.

But if his beautiful Eve thought he was going to let her throw herself away on a man like

Ethan Hayes, she was so wrong it actually hurt him to know that he was going to have to show her just how wrong she was. So what if the man was an outstandingly gifted architect? So what if he, Theron Herakleides, had actually held him in deep respect until today? By to-morrow Ethan Hayes would be out of the picture, Theron vowed very grimly, and Eve was going to learn to recover from her little holiday romance.

With those thoughts in mind, Theron turned away from the window to pick up the tele-phone. 'Ah—*yassis*, Leandros,' he greeted pleasantly, and fell into light conversation with his nephew while glancing back out of the window to see the way Eve had been left standing on the path, looking like a thoroughly whipped peasant instead of the proud and brave goddess he believed her to be.

Ethan Hayes would pay for that, he vowed coldly. He was going to pay in spades for play-ing with the heart of a sweet angel when every-one knew he was in love with Leona Al-Qadim!

'I am about to call in that favour you owe to me,' he warned Leandros Petronades, then went on to explain what he required of him. 'The sooner the better would be good for me, Leandros...'

Standing there on the sunny path, feeling as if she had just been reduced to dust by a man angry enough to tear down a mountain, Eve was carefully going over everything Ethan had tossed at her so she could be certain she had heard him correctly.

Aidan— 'Oh, good heavens,' she gasped as the whole thing began to get even more confused and complicated. Ethan believed it was Aidan, not Raoul, who'd been with her in her bedroom last night!

The telephone was ringing as Ethan let himself into the beach house. He stood glaring at the contraption, in two minds whether to ignore it. He didn't want to speak to anyone. He did not want to do anything but stew in the juices of his anger.

But, in the end, he gave in and picked up the receiver, if only to silence its persistent ring. It was Victor Frayne, his business partner, which did not improve his mood any. 'What do you want, Victor?' he questioned abruptly.

'Still as mad as hell at me, I see,' Victor Frayne drawled sardonically.

Mad as hell at the world, Ethan grimly extended. 'What do you want?' he repeated with a little less angst.

Victor went on to tell him that they had an emergency developing in San Estéban and that Leandros Petronades wanted Ethan back there to sort it out.

'Can't you see to it?' Ethan snapped out impatiently. He had no will to feel accommodating towards Victor nor Leandros Petronades for that matter, the latter being the spreader of gossip about his rich and varied love life!

'It's a planning dispute with the Spanish authorities,' Victor explained. 'Apparently we've breached some obscure by-law and they are now insisting we pull down the new yacht club and rebuild it somewhere else.'

'Over my dead body,' Ethan pronounced in fatherly protection of what happened to be one of his proudest achievements in design. 'We have not breached any by-law. I know because I checked them all out personally.'

'Which makes you the man with the answers, Ethan,' Victor relayed smoothly.

'Therefore, it makes this your fight. I have to warn you that they are threatening to bulldoze the place themselves if we refuse to do it.'

'I'll be on the next plane,' Ethan announced, and was surprised to discover how relieved he felt to reach that decision. Now he could get the hell out of paradise and leave the serpent to look for a fresh victim to mesmerise before she bit!

'Have you heard from Leona?' he then heard himself ask, and could have bitten himself for being so damned obvious.

'She's fine,' Leona's father assured him. 'She is cruising the Med as we speak and thoroughly enjoying herself, by the sound of it.'

Which puts me right in my place, Ethan thought as he replaced the receiver. Out of sight, out of mind and where I belong.

'Damn,' he muttered. 'Damn all women to hell.' And, on that profound curse, he picked up the telephone again with the intention of reserving a seat for himself on the three o'clock plane to Nassau, where he could catch a connecting flight to London, and then on to Spain. Only he didn't get quite that far because a movement at the door caught his eye.

CHAPTER SEVEN

SHE looked pale and fragile, as if someone had come along with an eraser and had wiped out all that wonderful animation which made Eve Herakleides the fascinating creature she was. His heart dipped. Had he done that? Or was the white-faced frailty Aidan Galloway's handiwork, and it was just that he had been too angry with her earlier to remember that she had been put through one hell of an ordeal only the night before.

No, he then told himself as a softening in his mood began to weaken his firm stance against her machinations. *Eve is trouble. You've done enough. Send her packing and get out of here.*

'What now?' he demanded in a hard, grim tone that told Eve he only had to look at her now to see trouble standing at his door.

But Eve wasn't Ethan Hayes' real trouble, she'd just come to realise. No, his trouble had been evident in the deep dark husky quality of his voice when he had spoken that other woman's name.

Suddenly she wanted to run, she wanted to hide, she wanted to pretend she had not over-heard his conversation, because she knew for sure now that Ethan had lied before, and he was tragically, painfully in love with Leona Al-Qadim.

At that precise moment she felt like trouble because she had this blistering urge to knock some sense into him! Would someone like to tell her, please, how a man like Ethan Hayes could allow himself to fall in love with a very married woman? Was she a witch? Had she cast a spell over him? Had they been such pas-sionate lovers that he'd been blinded by the sex and he couldn't see it took a certain type of woman to cheat on her husband?

No wonder the Sheikh had bruised his jaw for him! He deserved it, the fool! And she only hoped to goodness that the lovely Leona had received her just desserts too!

'Speak, Eve,' Ethan prompted, when she still hadn't managed to say anything. 'I'm in a rush. I have a plane to catch.'

A plane to catch, she silently repeated. Well, didn't that just about say everything else about him! Her eyes turned to crystal, backed by an ocean of burning green anger. 'So.' She stepped forward into his house and into his life with the grim intention to sort it out for him. 'You're going to leave the island and drop me in it because of one stupid phone call.'

The burning accusation flicked him like a whip. Ethan fielded it with the kind of small mocking smile that further infuriated Eve. 'That one stupid phone call was from my business partner informing me of an emergency that has developed on one of our projects in Spain,' he explained. 'And you dropped yourself in it,' he then coolly reminded her, 'by telling a pack of lies to your grandfather.'

'You had the chance to refute those lies. You didn't,' Eve pointed out. 'So now I'm afraid you are stuck with me.'

'As my future wife? Not in this life, Miss Herakleides,' he informed her. 'You know already what I think you should do, but if you still can't bring yourself to *drop* Aidan Galloway *in it* with your grandfather, then, with my speedy exit from here, at least you won't have to worry about me destroying your grandfather's trust in your honesty.'

With that cutting bit of arrogance he turned to walk away from this conversation—as if Eve was going to let him!

'Oh, you're so pompous sometimes.' She sighed as she trailed him across the sitting room. 'Do you ever stop to listen to yourself? I have no wish to be the wife of anyone,' she announced as she arrived in the bedroom doorway in time to see him settle a suitcase out on the bed. 'But, while we are on the subject of marriage, I'll point out that at least I am at liberty to be your wife if I wanted to be!'

The remark made him turn. Eve felt her skin start to prickle as she was reminded of wild animals again. 'Meaning—what?' he demanded.

She offered a shrug, that warning prickle forcing her to backtrack slightly. 'Meaning I don't have the wish, so why are we arguing about it?'

He knew she had backed out of what she had been going to say. It was there, written in the way she lowered her eyes from his—which in turn had his own narrowing threateningly. 'I don't know,' he incised. 'You tell me.'

His was an outright challenge for her to get off her chest whatever was fizzing inside it. He knew she knew about Leona. He knew she'd overheard his discussion with Victor just now.

But Eve was discovering that she just did not want to discuss his very married lover with him. She wanted to discuss *them*. 'Aidan Galloway,' she prompted, watching his face toughen up like a rock. 'I came here, because something you said on the path just now made me realise we seem to have been talking at cross purposes about what actually happened last night.'

Some of the challenge leaked out of him. 'He attempted to rape you.' Ethan named it.

'No.' Eve frowned. 'It wasn't—'

Ethan spun his back to her and walked over to the wardrobe to begin removing clothes from their hangers. 'Still protecting him, I see,' he drawled.

The comment stung. 'No,' she denied the charge. 'I don't need to protect Aidan. Not in this context anyway,' she felt pressed to add. 'And will you stop *doing* that and listen to me!' she snapped out, when he continued to pack his suitcase as if she wasn't even there.

Ignoring her demand, he made to walk back to the wardrobe. On a fit of irritation she went to stand directly in his path. She felt like a mouse challenging a giant and, the worst of it was, it excited her. Her insides came alive as if sparkling diamonds were showering her with the urge to reach out and touch.

'I am trying to tell you that Aidan Galloway was *not* the one who spiked my drink last night!' she told him furiously. 'You've been blaming the wrong man!'

Looking down into those rich green earnest eyes, Ethan had to wonder how such beautiful eyes could lie as well as they did? For some unaccountable reason the way she was still insisting on defending the bastard made him want to kiss that lying little mouth senseless.

Instead he released a very soft, very deriding laugh, took hold of her stubborn chin between finger and thumb and gave it a condescending shake. 'But you would say that, being so in love with him,' he taunted softly, then he sidestepped her and continued with what he was doing.

I knew I hated him, now I remember why,
Eve thought, and took in a deep breath of air
to give her the will to continue when really
she wanted to beat out an angry tattoo on his
back!

'We were at Aidan's beach house. It was my
birthday party and we were all enjoying ourselves…' Except for me, because I was brood-
ing over you! she added silently. 'Aidan was
the one who was mixing the drinks. But it was
not Aidan who slipped something potent into
my drink. It was *not* Aidan who brought me
home and—did what he did!'

'Who then?' he shot at her.

Ah, Eve thought, and snapped her lips shut.
Having seen his burning desire to rip Aidan
from limb to limb, she decided it might be
wise to keep the name of the real culprit to
herself for now. 'Who it was doesn't matter
any more.' She therefore evaded the question.
'I just needed to tell you that it wasn't Aidan.'

'You're lying,' he pronounced with a with-
ering glance at her.

'I'm not!' she denied. 'Aidan is one of the
nicest people I know!' she insisted in defence
of that look. 'And he's going through his own

bit of hell right now—so he doesn't need you accusing him of something he would not think of doing in a million years!'

'Are we talking about the same man who could lose himself in the embrace of another woman while his fiancée, his cousin and myself, looked on from the sidelines?' he mocked. Then on a sudden burst of impatience, he tossed the clothes he had been holding onto the bed and took a hard grip her shoulders. 'Stop protecting him, Eve,' he shook her gently. 'The man just isn't worthy of it!'

'I am telling you the truth,' she insisted. 'If you will just shut up and listen, I will explain about the kiss—'

'You're in love with him,' he repeated the outright accusation. 'That doesn't need explaining.'

'You're in love with another man's wife,' Eve retaliated in kind. 'What does that say about your right to moralise over me?'

His eyes began to darken ominously. Eve's senses began to play havoc with her ability to breathe or think. His mouth was hard and tight and angry, hers was soft and quivery and hurt. He was too close—she liked it. Her hands even went up to press against his shirt front. She felt his heat, the pound of his heart, the elixir of sheer masculine strength.

She wanted him to kiss her so very badly that it hurt.

Damn it all, but he wanted to kiss some sense into her, so badly it actually hurt, Ethan was thinking helplessly. 'He bruised your mouth, here,' he murmured, making do with running a finger over the soft smooth padding where the slight discolouration was still evident.

'She let her husband bruise yours,' Eve responded with a mimicking touch of a finger to the corner of his mouth.

He wasn't listening. 'And here,' he continued, moving that same gentle finger to the mark at her throat. 'I want to kill him for doing this to you.'

'It wasn't Aidan.' Somehow, some way she managed to hang onto a thread of sanity long enough to say that, even though she was becoming more engrossed in the pleasure of touching him.

'It wasn't Leona's husband who put the bruise on my face.'

'I still want to kill her just for breathing,' she confessed with enough green-eyed jealousy to make him laugh.

It was a strained, low, husky sound though, thick with other things, that made her insides begin to melt. Then he wasn't laughing. Instead he was taking her trailing finger in his and feeding it slowly into his mouth. Moist heat enveloped each sensitised nerve end, then spread right down to her toes. She released a soft breath of air and watched his steel-grey eyes turn to smoke. He was going to kiss her.

Yes, please, she begged him silently, and let him lower her hand back to his chest, let him lower his dark head, and parted her lips in readiness for when his met them.

Then he was kissing her, kissing her hotly, kissing her deeply, kissing her urgently like a man stealing something he knew he shouldn't take. But Eve wanted him to take. In fact she wholly encouraged him by sliding her hands up his shirt front until they joined at the back of his neck, then she parted her lips that bit more to invite him to take as much as he liked.

Heat poured from one to the other. One of them released a pent-up sigh—maybe both of them did. His hands left her shoulders and spread themselves across her slender spine, firm yet gentle in the way they urged her into closer contact with him. She liked it—loved it. This man had been threatening to ignite her like this from the first moment she had ever set eyes on him.

She was warm, she was sweet, she was seduction itself. She was everything he had been fantasising she would be for so long now he couldn't remember when it had begun. His hands felt enlivened merely by touching her. His body was slowly drowning in sensual heat. If she moved any closer, he'd had it, he was sure of it; that dragging sensation between his thighs was telling him he was ready to leap.

And the kiss? It just went on and on as a fascinating swim through a million pleasure zones. He didn't want it to end. Yet it had to end.

'What is this?' he murmured, against her mouth. 'Mutual consolation?'

He was trying to cool things, though Eve could tell he didn't really want to cool anything. So what if it was consolation to him? she asked herself. If the power of his hunger was anything to go by, Ethan Hayes was more than ready to be consoled. 'I'm game, if you are,' she therefore confided with enough breathy seduction to slay any man.

'Eve the flirt, Eve the temptress.' Ethan fought a hard battle between his desire to be tempted and a need to break free from her magic spell. But, in doing so, he hadn't realised he had said the words out loud.

Eve broke all connection. It was so abrupt he didn't even have time to respond. She turned away—walked away—then wrapped her arms around her body in a way he recognised all too well.

Eve trying to hug her pain away. He named it with a sense of bitter self-contempt for being the one to make it happen this time.

'I'm sorry,' he murmured. 'I didn't mean—'

'Yes, you did,' she cut in on him in a thin little voice.

A sigh eased itself from his body. 'All right,' he admitted it. 'So I think you like to tease men's senses.' She had been teasing his senses since the day they'd first met—was still teasing them! Even with whole chasms between them right now, he could still feel her lips and the impression of her body where it had pressed against his.

Damn it to hell! 'Aidan Galloway isn't the only man I've watched you turn inside out with a smile,' he added, angry with himself now for allowing that kiss to happen at all! 'Jack Banning isn't immune and neither is Raoul Delacroix.'

She stiffened sharply. 'Meaning what?' She spun on him. 'That I *did* get what I deserved last night?'

'I didn't say that.' Ethan sighed wearily. 'I will never say that!'

'But it's interesting that you're clocking up a whole list of men who could have been mad enough for me to want to spike my drink! We could even add your name, since you've just given in against your better judgement and kissed Eve the flirt!'

Ethan had no defence. 'I'm sorry,' was all he could say helplessly. 'But I was not making a judgement on you! If anything I was making a judgement on them! On me—it—oh, I don't know.' He sighed, heavily aware that he'd dug his own grave as deep as it needed to go.

'In other words the name doesn't really matter, just the one they revolve around,' Eve misunderstood him—deliberately he suspected.

'One name matters.' He grunted.

'As in, who tried the big seduction of Eve the flirt?' Ethan winced. Eve nodded, feeling that she'd more than deserved that telling wince. 'Well, let's go through all the candidates shall we?' She was beginning to warm to her sarcastic theme. 'We both know it wasn't you, so we can cross your name from the list. Jack Banning has a job to protect, so, even if it was him, he isn't going to come out and admit he so much as looked at me the wrong way. If it was Aidan, I'm in trouble because the Galloways are rich and powerful, and very clannish, they protect their own in ways you would not believe. As for André Visconte, he will defend his half-brother to his very last breath—as he has done on countless occasions before! Then there is my grandfather to consider—another rich man with too much power at his fingertips. If he finds out someone has dared to overstep the line, he will yell very loudly for the head of the man who tried to seduce his innocent granddaughter while she was under the influence of drink. War will be declared between the two involved families. But who do you think will come out of it with the damaged reputation? Me,' she threw at him. 'Eve the flirt. Eve the temptress. Eve the spoiled little rich girl who likes to lead men on for the fun of it and has finally received her just desserts!'

She was near to tears and didn't want him to know it, so she spun away again taking with her the image of him just standing there staring at her as if she'd just grown two heads. Well, maybe she had! She certainly felt as if she had two heads rocking on her neck. She was tired through lack of sleep, exhausted with lingering shock and whatever else was still permeating her bloodstream. And she was hurting inside because she still couldn't bring herself to understand why Raoul had believed he could do to her what he had tried to do! Nor could she quite manage to justify that she hadn't deserved what had happened.

That was the toughest pill to swallow. Self-contempt. She named it bleakly as she stared out of the window, while a deathly silence crowded in from behind. What was he thinking? she wondered painfully. What was now going on inside his cynical head?

Ethan was struggling to think anything much. She was amazing, was his one main impression, and that came from the gut not the brain. But, standing there with the light coming in from behind her, she seemed to shimmer like a proud goddess sent down from the heavens to mess up his life. No wonder her grandfather worshipped her. He was beginning to understand what that felt like.

He was also stunned by what she'd thrown at him. Worse, he wanted to refute what she'd predicted was bound to happen but knew that he couldn't. It was the way of the world. Since the beginning of time, woman had been cast in the role of temptress and man merely as a slave to her seductive wiles. He was as guilty as anyone of assuming the same thing about Eve. He'd even likened her to the serpent in paradise, when in truth the serpent had been his own desire to tap into that special magic that was Eve. Man being man at the expense of woman, in other words, blaming her for his weakness.

It was not a nice thing to admit about one-self.

'So...' He sighed in what he knew was his surrender to the whole darn package that was Eve. 'Tell me what it is you want to do,' he invited.

Eve turned to look at him. All he saw was a pair of tear-washed wounded eyes. 'Do you mean it?' she asked him in an unsteady voice that finally finished him.

Ask me to bite the apple, Eve, and I will do it, he mused ruefully, well aware that man's oldest weakness was still very much alive in-side him; after all he had just admitted to him-self. 'Yes, I mean it,' he confirmed and even felt like smiling at his own downfall.

Her fingers released their comforting clutch on her arms. He watched them lower to her sides then turn themselves into two tight, hope-ful little fists. He wanted to claim those fists. He wanted to prize those fingers open and feed them inside his shirt so they could roam at their leisure.

'Continue to play the charade—just for a few weeks,' she begged him. 'Give me time to let Grandpa down about this marriage thing—without my having to admit the truth to him.'

Well, he'd asked, now he knew. He was to play the love-struck lover of Eve until she decided it was no longer necessary. Why not? he asked himself. Why the hell not? At this precise moment he was even prepared to lie down on the floor and let her walk all over him.

Time to move, time to react. She was waiting for an answer. Dragging his eyes away from the inner vision of himself lying at her beautiful feet, he looked at his watch and tried to concentrate well enough to read it.

Twelve o'clock, he saw. 'You've got approximately two hours to pack a bag and say your farewells,' he announced with a smoothness that in no way reflected what was really happening inside him.

'Why, where am I going?'

Well, there's an interesting question, he mused. And wished he knew the answer. 'You can't come to despise me enough to jilt me while you're here in the Caribbean and I'm in Spain,' he pointed out. 'So you are going to have to come to Spain with me.'

CHAPTER EIGHT

EVE was late.

Standing by the car he aimed to return to the hire company at the tiny airport on the other side of the island, Ethan was beginning to wonder if she'd had a change of heart about coming away with him, when he caught sight of her coming along the path that led to the lane behind the beach houses.

She was pulling her suitcase behind her through the dappled sunlight cast by the shady overhang of the trees. Tall and slender, as always faultlessly sleek, gone was the sweet Miss Modesty look she'd created for her grandfather's benefit. Now the smooth and slinky siren was back in a misty-lavender skimpy camisole top edged with lace, and matching narrow skirt that did wonderful things to her figure as she moved. She had also let her hair down so it swung like spun toffee around her shoulders, and a pair of silver-framed sunglasses pushed up on her head held it away from her face.

A face that wasn't happy, Ethan noticed as she came closer. A face that was not just pale any more but sad and very grim.

'You're late,' he said as she reached him. 'I was beginning to think you weren't going to bother.'

'Well, I'm here, as you see.' And there was nothing loverlike, pretend or otherwise, in the way she flipped the sunglasses down over her eyes before she handed over her case then climbed into the car without offering another word.

Grimacing to himself, Ethan stashed the case then joined her. As they drove off up the lane he noticed that she didn't spare a glance for the sugar-pink gate posts that guarded her grandfather's property.

'He was okay about you leaving with me?' he dared to probe a little.

'Yes,' she answered, but he saw the tension line around her mouth and knew she was lying... Again, he tagged on, and wondered why it was that even the lies weren't bothering him any more.

'You surprise me,' he remarked mildly. 'Having flown in from Greece this morning specifically to spend your birthday with you, I expected him to be very annoyed that you were now walking out on him.'

'He didn't fly in from Greece, he flew from Nassau,' she corrected, 'where he always intended to return tomorrow, because his mistress is waiting there for him.'

Mistress. Ethan's opinion of the seventy-year-old Theron Herakleides altered slightly with that piece of information. 'I didn't know he had a mistress.'

'He has several,' his granddaughter supplied.

Ethan almost allowed himself a very masculine grin. 'Then, why not bring her here with him and save himself several island-hopping journeys?'

'A Greek male does not introduce his mistress to his family.'

'Ah.' Ethan began to see the light. 'And neither should a Greek woman introduce her lover to her family?'

'You are not my lover.'

'He thinks I am.'

'He also thinks you are only marrying me for my money,' she responded tartly. 'Says a lot about my personal pulling power, don't you think?'

It said a lot about his character too, Ethan noted grimly, and stopped the car. Turning towards her he viewed her profile through a new set of eyes, and released a heavy sigh. 'You fed him a very carefully constructed catalogue of lies to save his feelings and he disappointed you by not appreciating the gesture,' he deduced.

She didn't answer, but those hands were locked into fists again.

It made him wonder if she was having second thoughts about this and was being just too stubborn to admit as much. 'If you would rather stay,' he offered. 'I can understand if you—'

'No, you don't understand,' she suddenly flashed at him. 'And, like it or not, I am coming with you!'

'Then why are you so angry?'

'I am not angry,' she denied.

Reaching over, Ethan whipped the sunglasses from her eyes.

'Okay,' she conceded, 'So, I'm angry. Grandpa is angry,' she tagged on with telling bite. 'He was lying before when he appeared to be sanctioning our relationship. He now claims that there is no way he is going to let you marry me.'

'Good for him,' Ethan commended. 'It means he has your best interests at heart. I admire him for that.'

Her chin came up. 'Do you also admire him for setting up this so-called emergency in Spain, just to get you off the island and away from me?'

No, Ethan did not admire Theron for stooping that low. 'Are you sure about that?'

'He told me himself,' Eve confirmed.

'Oh, what a tangled web we weave…' Ethan murmured, then sat back in his seat with a sigh. 'Go back and tell him the truth, Eve,' he advised heavily. 'This has gone too far.'

'I will have my tongue removed before I will tell him the truth now!' she exclaimed. 'This is my life, Ethan! I have the right to make my own choices without interference from anyone!'

'So do I,' he announced with a sudden re-
solve that had him starting the car engine
again.

'W-what are you doing?'

'Going back,' he said.

'Why?' she challenged. 'Because you've
suddenly realised that he might decide to take
the Greek project away from you if you let me
step on that plane with you?'

Ethan stilled again. 'He threatened to do
that?'

Her mutinous expression gave him his answer. Without another word he turned the car
round and drove back down the lane and in
through the sugar-pink gate posts, then along
the driveway to pull up outside the palatial
frontage of the Herakleides holiday home.

He was angry now, burning with it. Getting
out of the car he walked round to open the
passenger door. 'Out,' he said, reaching down
to take hold of Eve's hand so he could aid her
arrival at his side.

'What are you going to do?' she asked.

'Call his bluff,' he declared. This was no
longer a case of helping Eve out of a situation.
It had become a case of his honour and integ-

rity being placed into question, and he didn't like that.

In fact he didn't like it one little bit.

Eve wasn't sure that she was looking forward to what was coming. It was one thing *her* being angry with her grandfather, but it was quite a different thing entirely to discover that she'd managed to make Ethan angry with him too. She loved that cantankerous old man. She understood where he was coming from; Ethan did not.

'Don't upset him,' she burst out suddenly.

Pausing in the process of closing the car door, 'Are you going to tell him the truth?'

He looked down at her, and she looked up at him, her heart flipped over. He was so much her kind of man that Grandpa couldn't be more wrong about anything! 'No,' she answered mutinously.

His dark head nodded. Her hand was grasped. He began trailing her behind him up white marble steps set between tall pink pillars. The front door was standing open; Ethan took them inside. The house was quiet, so their footsteps echoed on the cool white tiling as they trod the way across the huge hallway to

Theron's inner sanctum. The man himself was lounging behind his desk talking on the telephone. But the moment he saw them appear through the door, the phone call was severed and he was rising to his feet.

'So he brought you back. I expected as much.' The eyes of a cynic lanced Ethan with a dismissive look before they returned to his granddaughter. 'Which part did it, hmm? The part about me threatening to leave you nothing if he married you, or the part about the Greek project hanging in the balance?'

'Neither.' Striding forward with Eve still in tow, Ethan lifted up their linked hands and brought them down, still linked, upon Theron's desk. It was a declaration of intent, and Theron took it as such, his smug expression turning slightly wary as he looked at the other man.

'My submission for the Greek project is now formally withdrawn,' Ethan announced. 'Written confirmation will arrive on your desk as soon as I can have it typed up. As for your money—tell him Eve...'

Tell him Eve... Tell him what? A current of communication was running between them via those firmly linked hands, but for the life of her she didn't know what it was Ethan was expecting her say. Her grandfather was looking at her, Ethan was keeping his eyes fixed on her grandfather, and her mouth had gone dry as the idea sank in that Ethan was waiting for her to come clean with the whole nasty truth, so her grandfather would know then that this was all nothing but a terrible sham.

'Ethan doesn't want your m-money,' she began, having to moisten her lips with the tip of her tongue before she could find the will to speak. 'M-money isn't what this is about. He only w-wanted to—'

'Love a woman whom I think is worthy of being loved for herself,' Ethan took over. 'But you don't seem to agree,' he informed the older man. 'So while I provide written confirmation of my withdrawal from the Greek project, I suggest you protect Eve from my evil intentions and provide formal notice that none of your money can be accessed or offered in any way shape or form, to me.'

He meant it—he really meant it! 'Ethan—no!' Eve cried out. 'I can't let you throw away your livelihood because I—'

He kissed her to shut her up—did he kiss her! In front of her grandfather and without compunction, he kissed her until her knees went weak.

Theron watched that kiss, saw its passion, and felt its intensity like the pulsing beat of a drum. Eve emerged in a state of blushing confusion. Ethan Hayes was black-eyed, tight-jawed—and hot. If it wasn't for that troubling rumour about a certain married lady, Theron would be convinced that Ethan Hayes was as much in love with Eve as she clearly was with him!

But there was that niggling rumour, the old man reminded himself. Which then made him wonder if Ethan Hayes was executing one very convincing bluff here? Was he now expecting Theron to withdraw all threats, then sit back and think that all was right in his granddaughter's world?

'I will have all the relevant documentation drawn up and ready for you to sign when you reach Spain,' Theron announced, smoothly calling a double bluff.

It took the two lovers a long moment to respond. Their eyes were still locked, as were those dramatically clasped hands. Ethan Hayes stood one very handsome dark head taller that his sweet Eve, and Theron was willing to admit that they made a strikingly fetching pair.

'Why should I go to deal with an emergency that never was?' Ethan prompted.

Theron merely gave an indolent shrug. 'The emergency is real,' he confessed. 'The difference being that your business partner was attempting to deal with it himself without breaking into your holiday. Apparently my request for help to get you off this island merely tied in with what your people were already intending to do.' He even grimaced at the irony. 'So go and catch your plane,' he invited as a form of dismissal, 'for we have nothing left to discuss on this subject, other than to confirm that I will expect to see you both in Athens in two weeks for the formal announcement of your betrothal.'

Unless Mr Hayes had found a way to wriggle out of it by then, was the silent addition Theron kept to himself. Ethan Hayes was frowning down at him, unconvinced by his all-too easy climb-down. On the other hand, his beautiful Eve was breaking his heart with angry daggers for eyes.

'I don't want your money,' she announced.

Theron just smiled a silky smile. 'But you are getting it, my sweet angel,' he returned. 'Every single hard-earned drachma. And not one coin will be spent on him.' Theron looked at Ethan, bluff and counter-bluff stirring spice into his old blood. 'Perhaps you can recommend one of your competitors to take over the Greek project?' he intoned.

'You already had the best, and you know it,' Ethan countered. 'So be sure to inform Leandros that you've chucked me off the job. I can promise you that he is going to be absolutely ecstatic.'

With that neat and final arrogantly confident cut, Ethan turned to Eve. 'Say your goodbyes properly,' he commanded. 'I don't want you with me if you're going to be angry with him.'

Then he kissed her fully on the mouth again and strode away, leaving grandfather and granddaughter staring after him as if they could not quite believe he was real.

Ethan himself didn't know if he was real. He certainly felt different—alive, pumped up, energised, as if someone had slipped him the elixir of life.

That kiss with Eve perhaps?

Oh, shut up, he told himself frowningly. This is all just a sham, remember?

Just a great sham. Think of Aidan Galloway, he reminded himself. Whatever Eve liked to pretend, she had something going on with the Irishman. Love, sex—call it whatever—it was there, a throbbing pulse that said it was of a lot more than mere friendship.

'Watch him,' Theron advised, forcibly dragging Eve's attention away from the long, straight-shouldered stride of Ethan's retreat. 'He has your measure, my girl, and I don't think you are going to like that.'

Like it? She loved it. In fact it was tumbling around inside like a barrow load of sins desperately trying to get out. She wanted to run after him, take his hand again, laugh up into his arrogant face. She wanted to wind her arms around his neck and kiss him to heaven and back.

'You mean, *you* don't like it.' She turned a wry, knowing smile on this other man. She knew *he* had her measure, and wondered if he had guessed that all of this was just a sham?

A sham. Yes, a sham, she reminded herself, and felt the smile fade away like day turning to night. 'Grandpa—don't spoil this for me,' she heard herself say tremulously.

'He's dangerous,' Theron stated.

'I know.' Her eyelashes flickered. 'I like it.' It was a terrible confession to make.

'He is in love with another woman.' The reminder was supposed to be deadly to fragile emotions.

'I know that too.' Eve nodded. 'But he's what I want. I can make him love me instead of her, given a bit of time and space.'

'So this isn't just a ploy to bring poor Aidan Galloway to his senses about you?'

Aidan? Eve blinked. Her grandfather as well—? 'Aidan is still in love with Corin!' she protested, as if he had just suggested something terrible.

Theron took his time absorbing that declaration. It worried him, because if it wasn't Aidan, then this was exactly what it seemed to be. Yet his instincts were picking up all kinds of messages that conflicted with what he was

being shown here. He couldn't work it out. He
needed to work it out.

Getting up from his chair, he reached into a
drawer then came round the desk to stand in
front of Eve. In his hand he held a gaily
wrapped package. 'Happy birthday, my angel,'
he murmured softly as he fed the package into
her hands then placed tender kisses on both of
her cheeks.

He received his reward with the kind of un-
fettered shower of affection he'd come to expect from Eve. 'I love you, Grandpa.'

'I know you do, child.' And he did know it.
It was the substance his whole life had been
built upon since she'd been a shocked and
grief-stricken child of ten years' old. 'Now, go
catch your plane,' he told her. He had been
going to say go catch your man, but something
held him back.

Eve left with a promise to call him as soon
as she arrived in Spain. As the door closed
behind her, Theron was already reaching for
the telephone.

'Ah—*yassis*, Giorgio,' he greeted. 'I have a
job for you to do for me, my friend. Write this
name down: Ethan Alexander Hayes. *Ne*.' He
nodded. 'Anything you can find. Dig hard and
dig deep and do it quickly.'

CHAPTER NINE

Eve felt so stupidly shy when she settled into the passenger seat next to Ethan. 'Thank you for that,' she said a trifle self-consciously. 'I would have hated to leave him angry with me.'

Ethan made no response. Eve shot him a wary glance. His profile looked relaxed enough, but there was something about the shape of his mouth that suggested he was angry about something.

With her, with her grandfather, or with himself for allowing himself to become so embroiled in her problems?

The car engine came to life, the air-conditioning kicked in and began circulating cool air filled with the scent of him. His knuckle brushed her thigh as he shifted the gear stick. Suffocation seemed imminent, and Eve didn't know whether it was due to that so seductive scent, or to the sensation of his accidental touch which had left her body thickened.

Or maybe it had more to do with knowing that her grandfather was right. I'm letting myself in for a lot of heartache here, she mused. He doesn't love me, he loves someone else. Eve put a hand up to her trembling lips and felt Ethan's lips there instead. Her hand was pulled down again; it was trembling too.

'Say something, for goodness' sake.' The words left her lips on a shaken whisper.

Say what? Ethan thought frustratedly. I don't know what I'm doing here? I don't know what you are doing, coming away with me like this? You should be back there, home safe with your grandfather, because you certainly aren't safe here with me!

'What's in the packet?' Did he really just offer something as benign as that?

His fingers flexed on the steering wheel. The afternoon sunlight was shining on her bent head, threading red highlights through spun toffee like fire on silk. He'd never noticed the threads of fire before. Why was he noticing them now? Her skirt had rucked up, showing more thigh than he wanted to see. He could still feel the touch of her smooth skin against his knuckle and he wanted to feel more of it. All of it. Hell, damn it—everything.

'Grandpa's birthday present,' she answered huskily.

Husky was seductive. It was vibrating along almost every skin cell like a siren's melody. 'You haven't opened it.'

His voice had a rasp to it that was scraping over the surface of her skin like sand in a hot seductive breeze. 'He doesn't like me to open presents in f-front of him, just in case I don't like what he's chosen and he sees the disappointment on my f-face.' She was stammering. Stop stammering! Eve told herself fiercely.

She was stammering. Was she crying? Ethan couldn't tell because she had her head bent and her hair was hiding her face. 'Does it happen often?' Now he sounded husky, he noticed heavily.

'Never.' She shook her head. 'I always love anything he gives to me. You would think he had worked that out by now.' Another soft laugh and her fingers were gently stroking the present.

'Open it,' he suggested.

'Later,' she replied. She had enough to contend with right now without weeping all over Grandpa's gift as well.

They reached the top of the lane and turned onto the only proper road on the island. It went two ways—to the lane they'd just left, or to the small town with its even smaller airport, passing the entrance that led into the Galloways' bay on its way.

Two ways, Eve repeated. Forward, or back the way they had come. Did she want to go back? Did he want her to go back?

'Eve—if you've changed your mind about this, I can soon turn around and—'

'I'm coming with you!' The words shot out like bullets from a gun, ricocheting around the closed confines of the car.

Ethan snapped his mouth shut. His fingers flexed again. Eve sat simmering in her own hectic fallout, and silence reigned for the rest of the way.

It took ten minutes to get there. Ten long minutes of throat-locking hell. Eve gripped her birthday gift. Ethan gripped the wheel. They slid into a parking spot by the car-hire shop and both of them almost tumbled out of the car in their eagerness to breath hot humid air.

The nine-seat Cessna was waiting on the narrow runway. A porter ran up to collect their luggage to take it to the plane. Ethan appeared out of the car-hire shop, still feeding his credit card back into his wallet as he came. His dark head was bent, his hair gleaming blue-black against his deeply tanned face. He was wearing another blue shirt with grey trousers, and over his arm lay a jacket to match. Eve clutched at the strap to her shoulder bag, over which hung the cardigan that matched her top—and wished she didn't find the man so fascinating to watch.

He looked up. She looked quickly away. She looked beautiful, and his heart pulled a lousy trick on him by squeezing so tightly it took his breath away.

Nassau was a relief. They had a two-hour stopover, which meant they could both make excuses to go their separate ways for a while. Eve went window-shopping; Ethan went to hunt out somewhere he could access his website and download some documents so he could read them on the flight.

On his way back to find Eve, he spied a furry tiger with its tail stuck arrogantly in the air. He began to grin. Eve would never get the joke, but he couldn't resist going into the shop and buying if for her. While the toy was being gift-wrapped, he went browsing further down the line of shop windows and came back to collect the tiger with a strangely stunned expression on his face.

Eve was sitting with a fizzy drink can and a whole range of gifts packed into carrier bags. 'Souvenirs for my friends in London,' she explained. 'They expect it.'

Ethan just smiled and sat down beside her, then offered her his gift. 'Happy birthday,' he said solemnly.

She stared at him in big-eyed surprise. It was amazing, he mused, how much he adored those eyes. 'Open it,' he invited, tongue-in-cheek. 'I'm not at all sensitive to disappointment.'

He was smiling, really smiling, with his mouth, with the warm soft grey of his wonderful eyes. Eve smiled back, really smiled back, then handed him her can so she could give her full attention to ripping off the gold paper from her present. Meanwhile Ethan drank from her

can and watched with interest as the tiger
emerged.

There was a moment's stunned silence, an
unexpected blush, then she laughed. It was that
wonderfully light, delighted laugh he'd heard
her use so often for other people but never for
him before. 'Good old Tigger—you idiot.' She
turned to him. 'How did you know I have a
whole roomful of Tiggers back home?'

He hadn't known, but he did now, which
rather sent his private joke flat, because Tigger
was not quite the animal he had been thinking
about when he'd bought the furry toy. Still, did
it matter? She liked it, that was enough.

'ESP,' he confided, tapping his temple.

With her old exuberance, Eve leaned over to
kiss him, realised what she was about to do and
hesitated halfway there. Wary eyes locked on
his, and a black eyebrow arched quizzically
over one of them. Her heart gave a thud.
Irresistible, she thought. I'm falling head over
heels and don't even care any more. She closed
the gap, knowing by the dizzying curling sensation inside that a kiss was about the most
dangerous thing she could offer right now, even
here in the transit lounge of a busy airport with

hundreds of people playing chaperone...
Because he might think he was fatally in love
with Leona Al-Qadim, but he fancies the pants
off me!

And I'm available, very available, she added
determinedly. Their lips met—briefly—and
clung in reluctance to part.

Yes, Eve thought triumphantly, he does want
me. 'Thank you,' she murmured softly.

'You're welcome,' he replied, but he was
frowning slightly. Eve wished she knew what
thoughts had brought on his frown.

Thoughts of Leona Al-Qadim? Was he sitting here with one woman's kiss still warm on
his lips and daring to think of another? Like a
coin flipping over, she went from smiling cer-
tainty of her own power to win this man, to
dragging suspicion that the other woman would
always win.

Tigger was receiving a mangling, Ethan noticed, and wondered what the poor tiger had
done to deserve such abuse? Then he had to
smother a sigh, because he knew it was him
she was thinking about as she twisted the poor
animal's tail round in spirals. They kept kissing
when they shouldn't. They kept responding to

each other when they shouldn't. He was not the right man for her, and she was most definitely *not* the right woman for him.

'Here, do you want this?' He offered the drink can back to her.

Eve shook her head. 'You can finish it if you want.'

He didn't want it, but he knew what he did want. On that grim thought he got to his feet, too tense and restless to sit still any longer in this—crazy situation that should never have begun in the first place!

Walking over to the nearest waste-disposal bin he dropped the can in it, took a deep, steadying breath, then turned to go back the way he had come. Eve was no longer sitting where he had left her. Alarm shot through his veins like an injection of adrenalin, that quickly changed to a kind of thick gluey stuff that weighed him down so heavily he couldn't move an inch.

Why? Because her hair lay like silk against her shoulders, her bags of shopping hung at her sides. Tall and tanned and young and lovely, she was drawing interested gazes from every man that passed her by because she had class, she had style. She was an It girl, one of the fortunate few—and right at the present moment in time she was looking in the same jeweller's window he'd stood looking in only minutes before. Same place, same tray of sparkling jewels, he was absolutely certain of it. His feet took him over there, moving like lead in time with the heavy pump of his heart.

'Which one do you like?' he asked lightly over her shoulder.

She jumped, startled, glanced up at him, then looked quickly away again, blushing as if he'd caught her doing something truly sinful. 'The diamond cluster with the emerald centre,' she answered huskily.

Husky was back, he noticed, and husky he liked. Reaching down, he took her bags from her then placed a free hand to the small of her back. 'Let's go and try it,' he murmured softly.

'What—? But we can't do that!'

She was shocked, she was poleaxed—he even liked that. The lead weights dropped away from his body; he sent her a wry grin that made her eyes dilate. 'Of course we can,' he disagreed. 'It's tradition.'

Tradition, Eve repeated and felt her mind start turning somersaults, as the hand on her back firmly guided her into the shop. Ethan placed her bags on the floor at his feet, kept her close and calmly asked for the tray of rings. It arrived in front of them, sparkling beneath the lights. Long, lean, tanned male fingers plucked the diamond and emerald cluster off its velvet bed. While the assistant smiled the smile used for lovers, Ethan lifted up her left hand and gently slid the ring onto her finger.

'What do you think?' he prompted softly.

Eve wasn't thinking anything, she discovered. 'It fits,' was all she could manage to come up with to say.

'But do you like it?' he persisted.

'Yes,' she answered, so gruffly she didn't know her own voice.

'Good. So do I,' Ethan said. 'We'll take it,' he told the smiling sales assistant.

'But—look at the price!' she gasped as the assistant went away with Ethan's credit card.

'A lady doesn't check the price,' he told her dryly.

'But I can't let you buy something that expensive! Can you afford it? We shouldn't even be doing it.' Eve was beginning to panic in earnest now, Ethan noted, feeling his few minutes of pure romanticism turned to ashes as she spoke. 'W-we told Grandpa we were going to keep all of this a secret.'

'There will be nothing secret about us living together in Spain, Eve,' he dryly pointed out, and earned a startled look from those eyes for saying that. Yes, he thought grimly, take a moment to consider that part about us living together, Eve. 'But if you really don't want the ring—'

'No— Yes, I want it!'

'Good.' He nodded. 'A sham is not a good sham without all the right props to go with it.'

Eve's heart sank to her shoes as reality came rushing in. Here she was thinking—while he was only thinking—a sham. She swallowed on the thickness of her own stupidity. 'Then we'll go halves on the cost,' she decided.

If she said it to hit back at him then she certainly succeeded, Eve noted, as he stiffened. 'You really do think that because I can't match your grandfather's billions I must be as poor as a church mouse, don't you.'

Eve gave a noncommittal shrug for an answer. 'I just don't want you to be out of pocket just because I dumped myself on you like this.'

'Well, think of how much relief you will feel on the day you throw it back at me.'

The assistant arrived back to finish the sale then. Maybe it had been a timely interruption, Eve thought, as she watched him sign the sale slip and receive back his passport and credit card, because the sardonic tilt to his tone when he'd made that last remark had been aimed to cut her down to size. When, in actual fact, she suspected they both knew it was Ethan Hayes who'd taken the blow to his ego.

But the ring had suddenly lost value, its sparkle no longer seemed so fine. Their flight was called, and in the time it took them to gather up their belongings the whole incident was pushed away out of sight, even as the ring winked on her finger every time she moved her hand.

The plane was full, but first-class was quiet, with new state-of-the-art seating that offered just about every comfort that might be required. As they settled themselves in for the long journey, Eve unearthed Tigger from her hand luggage and sat him on the arm between their two seats.

You were my favourite birthday present, she told the stuffed tiger—not counting Grandpa's present, of course, she then added loyally, which she intended to open when she wasn't feeling so miffed at Ethan Hayes. As for you, she looked down at the ring sparkling like a demon on her finger, you're just a prop, which means you are as worthless as paste.

Within an hour of taking off, Ethan was deep into a stack of printed literature he'd managed to get someone in Nassau to pull off his website. Eve wasn't talking. Now he was glad he hadn't confided in her that the ring was the very one he'd picked out himself only minutes before she'd picked it out. Silly stuff like that provoked curious questions. Questions provoked answers he didn't want to give. It had been a stupid gesture anyway. He wished he hadn't done it. Now the damn ring kept on sparkling at him every time she turned a page of the magazine she'd brought with her onto the plane.

'Would you like a refill for that, Mr Hayes?' the flight attendant asked him. Glancing up at the woman he saw the look in her eyes was offering a whole lot more than a second cup of coffee.

Spice of life, he mocked grimly and refused the offer. As she went to move away he saw the flight attendant glance at Eve, then at her finger. That's right, he thought acidly, I've already been hooked.

By a toffee-haired witch with a sulk to beat all female sulks.

'And you, Miss Herakleides?'

'No, thank you,' Eve refused. And keep your greedy eyes off my man, she thought.

A man who had a way with a black ballpoint pen that held her attention with the same rapt fascination she would have given to Picasso if she'd had the opportunity to watch him at work. It wasn't as if he was actually doing anything special—just drawing circles round sentences then scrawling comments over the printed words. He was sitting back against the seat with an ankle resting across his other knee. He stopped writing, frowned, used the pen to relieve an itch on the side of his chin; he used it to tap out an abstract drum beat; he drew another circle, then scrawled comments again.

He sighed at something. His chest moved, and as she glanced sideways at it she realised she could see glimpses of deeply tanned flesh in the gaps between shirt buttons. Nice skin, warm skin, tight let-me-touch skin, she thought.

Close your eyes, Eve, and stop this! she railed at herself.

It wasn't long after she closed her eyes that the magazine began to slip from her slackened grip. Ethan rescued it and folded it away, then rescued Tigger as he too began to slip off his perch.

Tigger: fun, bouncy, always in trouble—he wasn't so old that he couldn't remember the animal's appeal. He had to smile at the irony because *his* tiger was neither fun nor bouncy, but it certainly meant to cause him a lot of trouble where Eve Herakleides was concerned.

Reaching over he gently placed Tigger on Eve's lap, then sent him a wry man-to-man look. 'Lucky guy,' he told the toy, and pressed a button that would recline her into a more comfortable position for sleep. A sigh whispered from her as she resettled her body. A glance at her eyes to check if he had disturbed her showed him the fine bruising around the sockets, which told him she was still suffering the effects of last night.

He'd forgotten about that. How had he forgotten about that? Because his mind had become fixed on more lusty things, of which he really ought to be ashamed.

He returned to his papers for a little while, but not very much later succumbed to the need to sleep himself. Halfway across the Atlantic he woke up to find that Eve had curled up on her side facing him, and her hand was splaying across his chest. But that wasn't all—not by a long shot because a couple of her fingers had somehow found their way into the gap between his shirt buttons and were now resting against his warm skin.

He liked them there, had no wish to move them, even though a call of nature was nagging at him. So he closed his eyes again and saw his own fingers slipping down the front of her gaping top in a quest to caress the warm golden globe he'd caught sight of as he'd glanced at her.

Then he thought. No way. He forced his eyes back open—just in case he might do in sleep what he had been fantasising about while

awake. Been there, done that once already today, he ruefully reminded himself. Instead he
gave in to the other desire and gently removed
her hand from his chest so that he could get
up.

She was awake when he came back, and her
seat had been returned to its upright position.
'Drink?' he suggested.

'Mmm.' She half yawned. 'Tea, I think, and
can you see if they can rustle up a sandwich?'

'Sure.' He went off to find a flight attendant.
When he came back Eve was not there and he
presumed she'd gone where he'd just been. She
slipped back into her seat as the flight attendant
arrived with a china tea service and a plate of
assorted sandwiches.

She'd freshened up, he'd freshened up, both
looked a bit better for it. Ethan poured the tea
while Eve checked the fillings between neat triangles of bread. 'Any preference?' she asked
him.

You, he thought soberly. 'I don't mind,' he
answered. 'I'm starving. We slept through dinner apparently.'

'You too?' she quizzed.

'Mmm,' he answered.

'Did you manage to finish your work before you slept?'

'Mmm,' he said again.

'Is that all you can say?' she mocked. 'Mmm?' It was like talking to a bumble-bee, Eve thought impatiently.

No, it wasn't all he could say, she discovered the moment he turned his head to look at her. Dark grey eyes locked with green, and the air was suddenly stifled by the kind of feelings that didn't belong in the cabin of an aeroplane. He wanted her. She wanted him. If they touched they would go up in a plume of fire and brimstone, it was so sinful what was happening to both of them.

They didn't touch. Eve looked away, picked up her cup and grimly drank the hot tea in the hope that it would outburn everything else. That damn ring flashed again and Ethan wished he hadn't put it there. It had been a mad impulsive gesture to make. This arrangement was a sham. The ring was a sham. But when he looked at that thing, Eve belonged to him.

CHAPTER TEN

THE rest of the flight was a lesson in how to avoid giving off the wrong kind of signals. They dropped down into Heathrow airport in the early morning local time, then had to hurry through transit to catch their connection to Malaga. That flight was full and noisy with excited children off on holiday to Spain. It was early afternoon by the time they cleared the formalities there.

Ahead of them lay a two-hour drive south to San Estéban, but one glance at Eve put the cap on that plan. Travel fatigue was casting a greyish pallor over her beautiful skin and she looked fit only to drop down and sleep where they stood.

Ethan had used a hand to guide her into a convenient seat in the airport arrival lounge. 'Sit,' he quietly commanded.

Subsiding without a single murmur, she watched him park their luggage trolley next to her through listless eyes and didn't even seem to notice that he then walked off without telling her where he was going.

He came back five minutes later to find her sitting more or less how he had left her. As he came to stand in front of her she looked up and, stifling a yawn, she pointed at their assorted luggage. 'Just think,' she said, 'how convenient it would be if we ever got married.'

Following the direction of her pointing finger, Ethan found himself looking at two sets of suitcases, both of which wore the same initials embossed on their leather like a sign from the devil of what the future held for them. He didn't like it. His mouth turned down in a show of dismay because those near-matching suitcases spoke of one giant step over that fragile line between, I can deal with this, and, The hell I can.

Eve saw he didn't like it. 'It was a joke, Ethan,' she sighed out wearily.

'Time to go,' was all he said—heavily.

Taking hold of her arm he pulled her to her feet when all Eve wanted to do was curl up in a dark corner somewhere, go to sleep and not wake up again while he was still in her life!

Then what did he do to throw that last thought right out of her head? He placed an arm around her shoulders, gently urged her to lean against him then kept her that close while pushing the trolley in front of them as they walked outside.

I like him this close, she confessed to herself. I love it when he makes these unexpected gestures of concern. 'You've no sense of humour,' she muttered in grim rejection of her own weakness.

'Or your sense of timing is lousy,' he suggested sardonically.

Maybe he was right. Maybe it hadn't been the most diplomatic observation to make when they were in effect walking alongside a whole pack of lies. She released a sigh; he acknowledged it by giving her arm a gentle squeeze that could have been sympathising with that weary little sigh. And, because it felt right to do it, she slipped her hand around his lean waist—and leaned just that bit more intimately into him.

As the automatic exit doors slid open for them, a small commotion just behind them made them pause and glance back to see a group of dark-eyed, dark-suited Spaniards heading towards the doors with a pack of photographers on their trail. It was only as the group drew level with them that Eve realised the men were clustered around an exquisite looking creature with black hair, dark eyes and full-blooded passion-red mouth.

'Miss Cordero, look this way,' the chasing pack were pleading. Camera bulbs flashed. Miss Cordero kept her eyes fixed directly ahead as her entourage herded her towards the exit doors Eve and Ethan had conveniently opened for them. As they swept by, someone called out to Miss Cordero. 'Is it true that you spent the night in Port Said with your lover, Sheikh Rafiq?'

Eve felt Ethan stiffen. Glancing up at his face she saw a frown was pulling the edges of his brows across the bridge of his nose. 'What?' she demanded. 'Who is she?'

'Serena Cordero, the dancer,' he replied.

Eve recognised the name now. Serena Cordero was the unchallenged queen of classical flamenco. Her recent world tour had brought on a rash of Spanish dance fever, causing schools dedicated to the art to open up all over the place. It wasn't just classical dance she performed with sizzling mastery. Her gypsy fire dance could put an auditorium full of men into a mass passion meltdown.

None of which explained why Ethan was standing block-still with a frown on his face, she mused curiously. Unless… 'Do you know her?' she asked him, already feeling the sting of jealousy hit her bloodstream at the idea that Ethan might know what it was like to have the exotic Serena dance all over him!

But he gave a shake of his dark head. 'I only know *of* her,' he said, making the chilly distinction.

'Then why the frown?'

'What frown?'

He looked down at her. Eve looked up at him. The now familiar sting of awareness leapt up between the two of them. 'That frown,' she murmured, touching a slender long finger to the bridge of his nose where his eyebrows dipped and met. It was too irresistible not to trail that fingertip down the length of his thin nose. Her hand was caught, gently crushed into his larger hand and removed.

The question itself was no longer relevant: Serena Cordero had suddenly ceased to exist. Mutual desire was back, hot and tight and stifling the life out of everything else.

'Let's go,' Ethan murmured, striving to contain it.

He wanted her, she wanted him. It was going to happen some time, Eve was sure of it. 'Okay,' she said.

Attention returned to the exit doors, they stepped outside into the afternoon heat. Coming here from the Caribbean should have meant they were acclimatised to it by now. But the Spanish heat was so dry it scorched the skin, whereas the Caribbean heat was softened by high humidity and cooled slightly by trade winds coming off the sea.

The Cordero entourage had disappeared already. There was a chauffeur-driven car standing by the kerb waiting for them. Eve was glad to escape into the air-conditioned coolness of its rear seat. Having helped to stash their luggage in the car boot, Ethan joined her. The heat emanating from his body made her shiver, though she didn't know why it did.

Two hours of this, she was thinking breath-
lessly, as they took off with the smoothness of
luxury. The prospect brought back the aching
tiredness, the tiredness thankfully dulled the
aching pulse of desire. Settling back into soft
leather, Eve had just reconciled herself to this
final leg of their journey when, to her surprise,
they hadn't even left the airport perimeter before they were turning in through a pair of
gates and drawing to a halt next to a gleaming
white helicopter bearing the Petronades logo
on its side.

'What now?' she asked curiously.

'Our transport to San Estéban, courtesy of
your cousin, Leandros,' Ethan sardonically
supplied. 'Having been so instrumental in getting us both here, I thought it was time he
helped make this final part a bit easier.'

Easier, truly said it. Their two-hour drive
south was cut by two-thirds. As they skipped
over the top of a lush green headland, Ethan
said, 'San Estéban.'

Glancing out of the window, Eve felt her
heart stop beating in surprise. 'Oh,' she said,
gasping in astonishment, unsure what it was

that she had been expecting, but knew that it certainly wasn't this.

Her gaze took in the modern example of a Moorish castle guarding the hill top, then it flicked down the hill to a beautiful deep-water harbour with its mosaic-paved promenade that linked it to the pretty white-washed town. In the quest to create something magical, that same Moorish style repeated itself in a clever blend of modern with ancient. Nothing clashed—nothing dared. It was no wonder that her grandfather had been so eager to have Hayes-Frayne apply their magic touch to his project, she realised. From up here she could see the same sense of vision that must have inspired her grandfather when Leandros had suggested he come out here and take a look for himself.

Turning her face she looked into Ethan's grey eyes and saw a different man looking steadily back at her. The artist—the man with the vision that inspired others; the sensitive romantic who perhaps could fall in love with the unattainable, and maybe even go so far as to love *because* that person was out of his reach. It was a well-known fact that artists liked to suffer; it was a natural part of their persona to keep the creative juices flowing by desiring what could never be.

Was that part of her attraction? Eve then found herself wondering curiously. With her grandfather openly stating that Ethan was not what he wanted for his only grandchild, had Theron unwittingly lifted her to the same desirable heights as the very married Leona Al-Qadim?

His eyes were certainly desiring her, she noted, but, for the first time, she didn't like what she could see. Don't raise me up onto a pedestal, she wanted to warn him, because she had no intention of remaining there, safely out of reach.

The helicopter dropped them onto a helipad custom-built to service the Moorish castle which, she realised, was really a hotel set in exquisite grounds. A car was waiting to transport them along the hill top that surrounded the bay where exclusive villas lay hidden behind screens of mature shrubs and trees. Eventually they pulled in through wide arched gates into a mosaic courtyard belonging to one of those villas.

Ethan unlocked the front door while the driver of their car collected their luggage and stacked it neatly by the door. Ethan knew the man; they'd chatted in Spanish throughout the short journey and continued chatting until the driver got back into his car and drove way.

Almost instantly silence tumbled down around them as it had done once before when they'd found themselves suddenly on their own like this.

'Shall we go in?' Ethan cut through it with his light invitation.

'Yes.' Eve made an effort to smile and didn't quite manage it as she walked into the villa while he brought the luggage inside then closed the door behind him.

Fresh tension erupted. Eve didn't quite know what to do next and Ethan didn't seem too sure himself, so they both started speaking at the same time.

'Is this one of your own designs?' she asked him.

'Would you like to freshen up first or—? No.' He answered her question.

'Yes, please.' She answered his.

He sighed, ran a hand round the back of his neck and looked suddenly bone-weary. Eve chewed nervously on her bottom lip and wished herself back in the Caribbean lying on a beach.

'Guest bedroom's this way...' Picking up her luggage he began leading the way over pale blue marble beneath arched ceilings painted the colour of pale sand. As they walked, they passed by several wide archways that appeared to lead to the main living space. But Eve was way beyond being curious enough to show any interest in what those rooms held. All she wanted was to be on her own for a while, to take stock, maybe even crash out on the large bed she'd caught sight of in the room Ethan was leading her into.

'Bathroom through that door,' he said as he placed her luggage on the top of a cedarwood ottoman. 'You can reach the terrace through there...' He pointed to the silk-draped full-length windows. 'Make yourself at home...' He turned toward the door, had seconds thoughts, and turned back again. 'I'll be working out on the terrace if you want me. Other than that...take your time...'

Lightly said, aimed to make her feel comfortable with whatever she wanted to do, he did not take into account that he hadn't once allowed his eyes to make contact with her eyes since they'd entered the villa.

Which meant that he was feeling as uncomfortable with this new situation as she was. 'Right. Fine,' she said.

He left her then; like a bat out of hell he got out of that room and made sure he shut the door behind him as he went. Eve wilted, had a horrible feeling that he was standing on the other side of that door doing exactly the same thing, and really, really wished she hadn't come.

Ethan was beginning to wonder if she'd made a run for it when, over an hour later, Eve still hadn't put in an appearance. At first he'd been glad of the respite, had taken a shower, had enjoyed a home-made pot of tea out here on the terrace with only the view and a dozen telephone calls to keep him company.

But as time had drifted on without him hearing a peep from Eve, he'd begun to get edgy. Now he felt like pacing the terrace because the tiger inside him was making its presence felt again.

What time was it? Six p.m., his watch told him. Two minutes later than it had been the last time he'd looked. He grimaced, then sighed to himself and walked over to the terrace rail to look down the hillside where San Estéban lay basking in the early evening sun. This time yesterday he had been sitting in the bar on the beach in the Caribbean drinking local rum and chatting with Jack Banning.

No, you were not, you were watching Eve dance with her eager young men and wishing you weren't there to witness it, a grim kind of honesty forced him to admit.

A sound further along the terrace caught his attention. His stomach muscles instantly tightened when he recognised the sound as one of the terrace doors opening. Eve appeared at last, wearing a plain straight dress with no sleeves, a scooped neck and a hemline that rested a quiet four inches above her slender knees.

Quiet—why quiet? he asked himself as he watched her walk over to the rail then stand looking out over the bay. There was nothing quiet about Eve Herakleides, not where he was concerned anyway. Her hair, her face, her wonderful figure— Even that sudden and unexpectedly shy expression on her face rang bells inside him as she turned and saw him standing there.

CHAPTER ELEVEN

'SORRY,' she murmured in apology. 'I fell asleep.'

'That's okay,' he replied, feeling all of that restlessness ease out of him to be replaced with—damn it—sex. The thought of it anyway. 'I've been working. Didn't notice the time.'

'This is a lovely view,' she remarked, turning her attention back to the bay. 'Nothing looks new or out of place; everything simply blends as if it's been like this for centuries.'

'That was the plan.' After a moment's hesitation he went to stand beside her and began to point out the different features the resort had to offer. She smelt of shampoo and something subtly expensive. Her voice, when she inserted a comment, played feather-like across his skin. 'We haven't even begun developing that area yet,' he said, indicating toward one of the farthest edges of the bay, and went on to describe what would be seen there within the next year or two.

His arm caught her shoulder, his voice vibrated along her flesh, raising goose-bumps on her skin as she listened to him—no—that she *absorbed* with a breathless kind of concentration every detail he relayed to her and wished she could remember a single one of them.

But she couldn't. It was the man who held her wrapped in fascination, the rest was just wallpaper pasted on for appearances' sake. 'Quite utopian,' she murmured eventually. 'And all your own?'

'No.' He denied that with a wry shake of his head. 'I would love to say it was, but a very austere Spaniard called Don Felipe de Vazquez owns all the land. Victor and I are just the men who transformed his ideas into reality.'

'All of this doesn't reflect an austere temperament.' Eve frowned. 'I see the heart of a romantic at work here.'

'Maybe he has hidden depths.' But, by his tone, it seemed he didn't think so. 'It's more likely he has a good instinct for what will return a healthy dividend on his land.'

'You don't like him,' Eve said, presuming from that.

'It's not my place to like or dislike him.' Ethan took the diplomatic line.

Turning against the rail, Eve folded her arms beneath her breasts then looked up at him sagely. 'But you don't like him,' she repeated stubbornly.

Ethan laughed, it was a soft dryly rueful sound that brought his eyes down to meet with hers. It was a mistake; the wrong move. Things began to happen to him that he had been determined he would not let happen. Don Felipe was tossed into oblivion; San Estéban with all its beauty may as well have not been there at all. Eve the witch, the beautiful siren, was all that he was seeing. She had relaxed with him at last, was actually smiling with her eyes, with her lovely mouth. Don't spoil it, he told himself. Don't so much as breathe in case you ruin the mood.

This wasn't easy, Eve was thinking. Maintaining this level of relaxed friendliness was tough when what she really wanted to do was kiss him so badly that it was like a fire in her brain. She'd fallen asleep thinking of this man, had woken up thinking of this man and didn't dare look into what had gone on in between.

Dreams were ruthless truth-tellers, she mused. 'Don Felipe,' she prompted, though she wasn't interested in the slightest in the Spaniard; it was important that she kept the conversation going, or she might give in and make an absolute fool out of herself.

His eyelashes flickered—long dark silky things that made her lips tingle as if they'd flickered against them. He took in a measured breath that expanded his ribcage and made her breasts sting into peaks. His mouth parted to speak but it wasn't what he was going to say that held her captive.

'You have to know a man to draw a considered opinion as to whether you like him or not...' Ethan dragged his eyes away from her before he did something he shouldn't. 'He's a strange man: very private, cold and remote. Rumour has it that he was disinherited by his father in favour of his half-brother, and didn't take the decision very well. Went a bit mad for a while, got into a couple of fights, had an accident, which left him scarred in more ways than one. Since then he has been out to prove something—with this resort and all the other investments he has made during the last few years that have earned him a fortune big enough to throw in his family's face. But does all of that make him a romantic?' His tone was sceptical to say the least.

'Then you must be the romantic at work here,' Eve announced decidedly.

Me—a romantic? Sending a fleeting glance over San Estéban, Ethan shook his dark head. 'I'm just an architect who likes to leave a place looking as untouched as it was before I arrived...'

Another silence fell. It had probably had to, because neither of them were really thinking about the discussion in hand. Words were appearing from within the mists of other things.

'Drink,' Ethan said, filling the gap again.

'Yes,' she agreed. Relieved to have an excuse to move, she straightened away from the rail at the same moment that Ethan shifted his stance and made the fatal mistake of looking down at her. That was all that it took to flip the mood right into that one place they'd both been trying to keep away from. Eve saw his eyes dilate, saw the breath grow still in his chest. Her smile began to die along with her relaxed manner, because she knew for certain now what was really going on inside his head.

His tension began to fight with hers. 'And food,' he added. 'We need to eat. The kitchen is stocked with all the usual provisions, but we can eat out if you prefer.'

Eat in or out? Eve tried to make a decision, found she couldn't because sexual desire lay too thickly in the atmosphere to think of anything else. It would take only one more move, one tiny gesture from either of them, to lick desire into a flame.

'In,' she said, choosing. 'I've had enough of crowded places for one day.' She even managed to send him a semblance of a smile to accompany the reply.

But the smile was the gesture. It made him look at her mouth. Eve released a soft gasp as if she'd just been surprised with a kiss. The flame was licked, her arms unfolded and he was taking their place. They went into each other's arms without another sane thought, and all it took was the first light brush of their lips to plunge them right back to where they'd cut off on the plane over the Atlantic.

Hungry and hot, it was the kind of kiss that worked on every sense until she was trembling so badly she needed to hang onto something. That something was his neck where the tips of her fingers had curled and had dug in. And he was no better, taking what she offered with an urgency that fed the need. His hands explored her body, his touch sure with knowledge, sensually driven by man at his most practiced: He was not the fumbling boy Raoul had been the night before, a slave to his own urgent needs.

Eve knew the difference. And so Ethan should have understood that—being the sophisticated lover he was reputed to be. But he shot back so abruptly it was like being severed at the neck. 'What am I doing?' He began cursing himself. 'Great move, Ethan,' he told himself harshly. 'Great damn move!'

'You started it!' Eve threw at him as if he'd implied otherwise.

It swung him round. 'Do you think I don't know that?' he tossed back harshly. 'You suffered a bad experience only yesterday. If I took advantage of you now, it would make me no better than the bastard who did that to you! I apologise,' he clipped out. 'If I ever attempt anything like that again you have my permission to cry—'

Rape, Eve finished when he so obviously couldn't. And there it was, she realised. In one ill-thought-out sentence Ethan had brought this whole ugly situation back to where it really belonged.

So it is me who makes this happen, she realised. You don't get two men in one day thinking you're open to that kind of thing without you giving off something that tells them that!

'You're wrong, so stop thinking it,' he said.

'Why wrong?' He had to explain that or it meant nothing!

Ethan made himself look her in the eyes, made himself take the slap of those pained tears that glittered there. 'You wanted me,' he explained. 'You did not want him.'

It was true. Was it true? Too shaken to think straight, she looked away from his grim hard face, and down at her body where she could still feel the lingering pleasure of his touch. With Raoul she'd felt revulsion, only revulsion. But that didn't mean she hadn't *asked* for what he'd tried to do! Did it make a difference that she hadn't known she'd been doing it? No, it did not. A flirt was a flirt. A tease was a tease. She looked back at Ethan through pain-bright eyes filled with a terrible self-disillusionment.

'No,' he denied, knowing what was raking around inside her head. 'No!' he repeated and walked back to take her by the shoulders and issue a gentle shake. 'With him, you screamed, Eve,' he pointed out gruffly. 'Even under the influence of whatever he gave you, you screamed loud enough to waken me.'

But that doesn't mean I didn't bring it on myself! she thought painfully.

'You're beautiful, stunning—irresistible in many ways,' he went on as if he could read the thoughts tumbling through her head. 'But ninety-nine per cent of the male population will resist you—unless you don't want them to.'

And I did not want you to resist me. 'But you stopped it anyway,' she whispered shakily.

'Because it was wrong. Because it is not what we're here for.'

'You pompous swine,' she said and turned to walk back to her room.

She didn't get very far. He exploded so spectacularly it came as a shock. 'What is it you actually want from me, Miss Herakleides?' he roared at her furiously as he strode towards her. 'I thought you wanted my help, so I gave it.' His hands found her shoulders. 'I thought you wanted my support with your lies, so I gave you that!' Those hands spun her round to face the fury he was giving out. 'You're here. *I'm* here, living a lie that should never have been allowed to start in the first place!' Cold steely eyes raked her face like cutthroat razors. 'Now I can't even honour that deal without you making me out to be some kind of rat!'

'I didn't mean—'

'Yes, you did,' he cut in thinly.

'I thought—'

'You don't think, Eve, that's your trouble!'

'Will you stop shouting at me,' she yelled back. 'I wanted what I thought you wanted! My mistake. I apologise. Now let go of me!'

He did. She staggered. His hands came back to steady her. She released a pathetic little sob.

He muttered something. She looked up at him. Like lightning striking a volcano, a whole ocean of molten emotion came boiling out.

'He was there; he hurt me. You were the last person on earth I expected to understand! I liked it—your kindness, your caring, the strength that you let me lean on.' Stop trembling! she told herself. 'I liked the way you could be so stern with me, but make love to me with your eyes at the same time. You're doing it now!' she choked out shrilly. 'You're angry but you want me. I am *not* misreading the messages! How dare you imply that I am?'

It was a damning indictment. She was right, every word of it. Standing there, watching this beautiful woman shimmer with anger, hurt and a million other emotions beside, Ethan took it all full in the face and wondered what he was supposed to say or do now.

Then, he thought, oh to hell with it. He even released a short laugh because he knew what he was going to do with it. He was going to throw off his high moral stance and surrender to Eve—as he had been doing since this whole crazy thing had begun.

'Don't laugh at me,' she protested unsteadily, hurt tears sparkling across dark green irises.

'I'm not laughing at you,' he denied. 'I'm laughing at myself.'

'Why?'

Ethan kissed those tear-washed eyes, ran his lips down her cute little nose and settled at the corner of her trembling mouth. 'Because of this,' he murmured huskily, and made his surrender, falling into it without allowing himself another sane thought.

'If you're playing games with me, I'll—'

'No game,' he promised and, because they'd done enough talking, he moved his lips until they'd covered her own then gently parted them to receive the moist caress of his tongue.

It was different. Eve could feel it was different. Not just the kiss but the way he was holding her—not with anger nor that driving compulsion that had pulled their mouths together before. He was going to take what she had placed on such open offer, and for a fleeting, fleeting, moment Eve wondered if she had made a terrible mistake by making herself so easy for him. Then he lifted his head, and she saw the slightly awry smile he offered that told her he wasn't thinking this was easy at all.

'Beautiful Eve,' he murmured and covered her mouth again, picked her up and carried her down the terrace, into her bedroom and over to the bed before he let her feet slide down to the floor.

Shy, she felt agonisingly shy suddenly, which was stupid after everything that had gone before. He cupped her face, felt the burn in her cheeks, brushed his thumbs across them gently and felt her small tremor as he tilted her head back enough to receive his next kiss.

Only, not just a kiss but a deep and desirous prelude to what was about to come. It was a warm and unhurried awakening of the senses that held her captivated and compliant, wanting to go only where he led her.

He noticed, of course he did. 'A passive Eve?' he mocked her gently.

'Yes,' she whispered. 'Do you mind?'

'No.' But that awry smile was on his lips again. 'Just so long as it doesn't mean you're having second thoughts and don't know how to tell me.'

'No second thoughts.' And to prove it, she wound her arms around his neck and brought his mouth back to hers again, then mimicked his long seductive kiss.

He led her through an erotic undressing by drawing the zip of her dress down her spine with caressing expertise that took her breath away. His fingers trailed feather-light over exposed skin, sun-kissed shoulders, slender backbone, the shockingly sensitised concaved arch at the nape of back. She moved against him and could tell that he liked that. It emboldened her into pressing the bowl of her hips even closer to what was happening to him.

He released a sigh; it shook with feeling. Eve matched that too, and he caught the sound on his tongue then fed it back to her, while his hands drifted up her arms until they reached her hands still locked around his neck. Drawing them downwards he encouraged her dress to slither down her body, then laid her hands against his shirt front. 'Undress me,' he urged.

It was the calling song of a mating bird. Shy though she still felt, Eve complied, while the caress of his hands and his mouth urged her on. Did he know? she wondered mistily. Could he tell she'd never done this before, and was that why he was taking it all so slow and easy?

Shirt buttons slid from their buttonholes to reveal more and more of that wonderful chest she loved to look at so much. Now she allowed herself the pleasure of touching, placing her fingers on his chest where dark hair coiled into the hollow between tight pectoral muscles. Then, because she couldn't resist, the moist tip of her tongue followed suit.

The air left his lungs on a heavy rush that brought her head up sharply. She looked up at him, he looked down at her, and the pace suddenly altered dramatically. They fell on each other's mouths with a series of deep hot hisses while his urgent hands stripped her flimsy scrap of a bra away and hers pushed the shirt off his back.

Then it was flesh on flesh, pleasure tangling up with pleasure as the whole thing shot off on its own natural journey. His arms were crushing her, his kiss was deep, their laboured breathing hissed into the warm golden light of the slow-dying day as he manoeuvred her down onto the bed. He came down with her, his skin was moist, she yearned to taste it but the kiss was just too good to break away from. His hands began caressing her with so much sensual expertise that she arched and flexed as sensation washed over her in waves and scraped restless fingernails over his shoulder blades with enough urgency to make him shudder in response.

'Sorry,' she whispered helplessly.

He released a thick laugh and said, 'Do it again.'

The exchange of words broke the kiss. Without the kiss she was free to indulge herself by tasting him. He liked her nails so she ran them down his back, loving the feel of his muscles flexing pleasurably, loving the groan he uttered just before he claimed one of her breasts with his mouth.

Desire stirred and writhed like an unleashed serpent deep within her abdomen. He must have known, because his hand was suddenly playing her stomach, moving downward, fingertips slipping beneath the scrappy fabric of her briefs. She knew he was going to touch her, knew that this was it, the moment she had been waiting for for what seemed the whole of her life. A tight and tingling breathtaking anticipation sent her still, which made him lift his head and send her a sharp questioning look.

'What?' he said.

'You,' she said in a sexually tense little voice.

He understood. His eyes went black, his features tightening into a very male, passionate cast. The hand slipped lower, fingertips drifting through dusky curls to seek out warm moist tissue that was the centre of her world right now. She groaned then gasped as pleasure licked with stunning intensity through to her toes and fingertips. He murmured something she didn't hear—it could have been her name or it could have been a curse because she knew she was rocketing right out of control here.

He encouraged her though. With the mastery of the seasoned lover, he orchestrated her pleasure trip through the senses. Did he know? He had to know. Surely no man took this much care to please the woman he was making love to without expecting some similar stimulation back by return, unless he knew that this was her first experience?

The last of her clothing was trailed away; she was vaguely aware of him ridding himself of his own. When his hands were busy elsewhere his mouth took up the burning seduction of her breasts, her navel, brushing hot moist kisses along the inner surface of her golden thighs.

Flesh burned against flesh; long restless limbs tangled in a love-knot caress. They rolled. He came above her, her hands locked around his neck. It was then that she felt the probing force of his masculinity and as her insides curled in anticipation she uttered his name on a sensual breath.

He liked it; she felt his response in the small shudder that ripped through his body. She liked that, and responded with a lithe flexing of her hips that made her exquisitely aware of the power he was still keeping in check.

'Eve, give me your mouth.'

She gave him her mouth, willingly, hungrily. She gave him every little bit of herself that she could possibly give. He took it all. Like a man leaping into a fiery furnace knowing he was about to get severely burned, he made a single strangled sound in his throat then, swift and sure, he claimed the passage he had prepared for himself.

It was wild, it was shocking, it was shamelessly exhilarating. Barriers broke; she winced on a soft little gasp. He paused, touched her cheek with unsteady fingers, gently combed her hair away from her face.

'Eve,' he breathed.

She opened her eyes and made contact with the burning black density of his. He looked different, darker, masculine, more her man than ever.

'Yes,' she breathed, closed her eyes again, then made a single stretching movement that fastened her to him as a whole new hot probing journey held her in its spectacular thrall. He took her to places she hadn't known existed; he taught her things about her that held her trapped on the pin-piercing pinnacle of discovery for long agonising seconds before he tipped her over the edge with the sudden increased rush of masculine thrust. She learned what it was like to lose touch with everything but a swelling pulsing pleasure of the senses.

When it was over it was all she could do to hang onto him while he lay heavily on top of her with their pounding heartbeats throbbing all around.

He went to move. She stopped him. 'Wait,' she whispered. She didn't want to miss a single sense-soaring moment in this act of momentous importance to her. She had waited so very long for this to happen, had never been slightly tempted to experiment because she had been so determined to wait for the right man to come along—the one she would know instinctively was the one man for her. Marriage, wedding gowns, playing the shy virgin bride had never come into her perfect dream. It had just had to be the right man. She'd found that man, and nothing—no moment in time—was ever going to feel as special as this.

CHAPTER TWELVE

EVE'S sigh was soft against his shoulder; it whispered the pleasure still permeating her blood. Ethan knew the feeling; it was with him also. But that didn't mean he was feeling good about this.

What had he done—?

What the hell had he done? He didn't deserve this, he did not deserve one half second of what she had just given to him. Now he was desperate to move, to separate from this incredible creature so that he could take stock—come to terms with what this was going to mean to the both of them.

He felt her begin to stir beneath him. It became the most sensually evocative stretch of the female body that began at her shoulders and arched her slender spine and flexed the cradle of her hips where he received the full kick of the movement because they were still joined.

At least with that stirring she also gave him permission to move by slackening the grip her arms had around him. Using his forearms as braces to take his weight, he levered himself away from her, and shuddered at her soft quivering gasp as he withdrew other parts. The gasp didn't surprise him. He might be wishing himself a million miles away at this precise moment, but his body certainly wasn't agreeing.

It wanted more—already. It wanted him to begin the whole wildly exciting process all over again.

'Say something,' she murmured.

The soft sound of her voice brought his head round to look at her. She was lying there beside him with her cheek resting on her forearm and gazing at him through shy, dark, vulnerable eyes. His heart pitched and rolled. She looked gloriously, stunningly, *achingly* lovely with her hair spreading out across the pillow and her face wearing that satiated bloom.

'I was your first lover.' It was the only thing rattling around his head that was fit to be said.

The bloom deepened, her eyelashes flickered down in a bid to hide away from that soul-blazing truth. But not for long; not this woman who had so much spirit; she wasn't going to let a bit of shy self-consciousness beat her. So the lashes rose up again, gave him a view of deep green, slightly mocking, eyes packed full of the new knowledge he had given to her. 'Thank you for making it such a memorable experience,' she said softly, and smiled.

That smile... He felt it reach right down inside and grasp hold of certain parts. The urge to roll towards her and recreate the whole magic again was so tantalising he could actually taste it.

Or taste Eve, he amended grimly, and sat up. 'You should have told me,' he censured.

There was a moment's silence, a moment's total stillness, a moment in which he felt muscles clench all over him because his gruff, curt attitude had just wiped the pleasure right out. He felt it leave like an actual entity, unfolding itself from their flesh and slipping silently through the open terrace window.

Not Eve though. She still lay beside him; he could see her slender bare feet, the sensual curl of her toes and the gold silk length of her slender legs.

'Why?' she challenged. 'Is there some un-written rule somewhere that says all first-timers must announce that fact before proceeding?'

Put like that, he wanted to laugh. But the bottom line still read like ten vicious swear words. 'I had a right to know.'

'You believe you had a right of say over my virginity? Rubbish,' she denounced. 'For what purpose?' she demanded. 'So that you could make the decision as to whether you wanted to take it or not?'

'No.' This, Ethan realised, was not going to be easy.

'Then, what?'

The silky gold legs disappeared from his vision, the slender feet, the sensually curling toes. His eyes followed them as they slid across smooth white sheeting to snake out of his sight as she pulled herself up—not to sit but to kneel somewhere behind him. He felt her rise upwards, smelt the sweetly seductive scent of her skin, felt her sigh brush his nape, just before her arms appeared over his shoulders and long delicate fingers with nails painted hot-pink came to rest in the hair matting his chest. Her lips caught his ear lobe, her teeth gently bit, and sensation sprinkled through him like a thousand pinpricks, the tips of her breasts pressing like two hard buttons against his back.

'It wasn't your special moment, it was mine,' she told him. 'Go all Neanderthal on me and I might not let you teach me how good it can be the second time…the third…' She bit his lobe again. 'To infinity and beyond,' she whispered sensually.

His short huff of amused laughter found voice this time. Eve the flirt, Eve the temptress, Eve the serpent in paradise, whom he seemed to have transported with him across half the world. Now it was Eve the dangerous seductress. Though she might have just enjoyed her first experience in making love, even now he knew he could teach her nothing. She was a natural, born to it. Special and rare.

What had that small burst of laughter been for? Eve wondered anxiously. Was he thinking she was incorrigible? Was he thinking she must be a real little hussy to make so light of what they'd just done?

But Eve didn't feel light about anything. She was worried. She was scared in case he took the honourable path and decided her virginity came with a price tag he might be forced to pay, when all he'd really been doing had been giving in to the temptation she'd so blatantly thrown his way.

She loved him, she wanted him, but not without him loving and wanting her above anything else.

Anything? she then questioned. One woman, she amended. One unavailable woman, who had no right to keep the heart she could never cherish. Well, move over, Leona, she thought possessively. Because you've just lost out and this beautiful man's heart is going to belong to me!

'I need a shower,' she murmured huskily against that tasty ear lobe. 'And so do you.'

Invitation—demand. Ethan stared down at the place against his chest where his ring winked defiantly up at him. She's all yours, mate, it seemed to be telling him. For now at any rate.

Well, to hell with it—why not? he decided. He was a big boy, he could take it when it was

over and it was time to get out! So he turned
to look at her, dislodging her arms in the process so she sat back on her haunches looking
at him through wide green wary eyes. She
wasn't sure what was coming but he knew.

He looked her over, his eyes stripping off a
layer of skin with their silver-bright possessive
blast. Then he swung himself off the bed,
turned, and pressed Eve up against his chest
so that her eyes were level with his and her
thighs were clinging to his narrow waist. 'Your
grandfather,' he said, 'should have locked you
away years ago.'

She grinned; her eyes began to shine; she
had the audacity to put out her tongue and lick
the shape of his mock-stern mouth. 'Jack
Banning said the very same thing,' she informed him. Then before he could respond,
she kissed him—hell, did she kiss him! She
kissed him all the way into the adjoining bathroom, then the shower and, as promised, beyond.

Eve was in the kitchen and was humming to
herself as she waited for the toast to pop up
from the toaster. Sunlight was pouring in
through the open door which led onto the ter-

race and behind her lay the remnants of the meal they'd eaten in here the night before—though for the life of her she couldn't remember what that meal had consisted of.

It didn't matter. Nothing mattered, other than for the huggable knowledge that she had spent the night in Ethan's home, in Ethan's bed, in Ethan's arms, making wonderful love. She was now wearing Ethan's shirt as she prepared his breakfast, while his voice filtered into her from out on the terrace where he was sounding very smooth, very slick, very informed as he spoke in fluent Spanish to some authoritative body. She loved his voice; she loved its rich deep texture and what it did to her tummy muscles as she listened to him. She loved this feeling of complete contentment as she prepared breakfast for him.

He stopped talking as the toast popped up, his footsteps sounding on pale blue tiling as they brought him into the kitchen to look for her. She smiled as his hands came to cup her hips, crushing fine cotton against her cool flesh. 'Mmm, that smells good,' he said, then buried his mouth in the side of her throat.

It really was quite sinful the way she responded, turning round in his grasp to demand that mouth for her own. His hands shaped her body and hers stroked the smooth clean surface of his freshly shaved face. Things would have moved onto something else if the telephone hadn't started ringing.

He was reluctant to let her go, Eve equally so. But she liked the evidence of frustration in his eyes as he dug his mobile out of his pocket and placed it to his ear.

'Ethan Hayes,' he announced in that deep smooth drawl that made her toes curl into the floor. He was wearing a light grey suit, white shirt and grey tie and was looking dynamic, again, she noticed with a wry little smile as she turned back to the toast while he discussed local by-laws.

The call ended just as she finished slotting triangles of toast into a toast rack. There was a short sharp silence that alerted her before she even turned round and saw his face.

He was gazing ruefully at the breakfast tray she had prepared ready to take out onto the terrace. 'You're going to be angry with me for this,' he warned her. 'But I'm afraid I'll have to miss breakfast. I have a meeting in ten minutes down at the yacht club.'

Disappointment curled inside her tummy but she kept it from showing on her face by hiding it behind an understanding smile. It was what he had rushed back here to Spain for, after all. 'So much for my display of domesticity,' she mocked.

'I shouldn't be long,' he assured her. 'You'll be all right here on your own until I get back?'

'I'll try my best not to go into too deep a decline while you're gone,' she promised.

'What about my decline?' he countered quizzically.

It was nice of him to say it, but he was in no danger of wasting away from not having her within touching distance. He was already pumped up and eager to go and take on the whole Spanish government.

Folding her arms beneath her breasts, Eve leaned against the worktop and sent him a dry look. 'Go,' she said.

'Right,' he said, but still didn't move. Instead he looked at her, really looked at her, with a slight tilt to his head and a slight frown to his brow, as if he was trying to work something out about her but couldn't quite grasp what that something was. Then he seemed to give up on it and, with a brief smile, he brushed a kiss across her cheek. 'I'll be as quick as I can,' he said.

Then he was gone, striding out of the kitchen and away from her with his car keys jangling in his hand as he made for the rear courtyard, where she'd noticed the set of four garages when they'd arrived the afternoon before.

Left on her own, breakfast lost some of its appeal, though the aroma of fresh coffee was too inviting to ignore. So she carried the tray out onto the terrace and sat at one of the tables there to drink it and watch San Estéban glitter with the early morning crystal-clarity that came with the promise of a perfect summer's day. After that she spent some time tidying the kitchen, then decided to take a long shower and dress before exploring the rest of the villa, since she hadn't bothered to notice anything much the day before.

She took the terrace route to her bedroom, noticed she hadn't even got around to unpacking her suitcase, and wondered if Ethan had unpacked his? A quick shower and she was just slipping into a short blue skirt and a white sun top, her next intention to explore the villa, when a telephone began ringing somewhere, it was the land-line kind that announced itself as such by its distinctive tone.

Ethan? she wondered, and felt her heart leap. He had only been gone a couple of hours yet he was missing her so much he had to give her a call? Hurrying out of the bedroom, she began to follow the sound down the wide arched hallway. The villa suddenly felt big and empty, and she wasn't sure she liked Ethan's taste in décor. It surprised her to think that because she liked just about every other thing about Ethan, she mused with a smile as she walked between pale sand walls on the same pale blue tiling that seemed to cover the floors throughout. It was all very cool, very Lawrence-of-Arabia, nothing shouted, nothing scarred the eyes. Yet...

She found the telephone in one of the reception rooms. As she moved towards it, it suddenly stopped ringing and the answering machine kicked in. As she waited to hear if it was indeed Ethan trying to contact her before she decided to pick up the receiver, she began to look around the room.

A stranger's voice suddenly filled the air space. Deep and smooth, it possessed the same rich English tones as Ethan's voice, only it lacked his toe-curling attraction.

'Ethan,' the voice said. 'It's Victor. When you get a spare minute, give me a call. I'm at the London office and that cantankerous devil, Theron Herakleides, has decided to go silent about the Greek project.'

Grandpa. Eve smiled at the cantankerous description, frowned at the part about the Greek project because she'd forgotten about her grandfather's threats. She remained standing there waiting for Victor Frayne to finish his message so that she could call up her grandfather and try and convince him he would be cutting off his nose to spite his own face if he pulled Hayes-Frayne's submission.

Maybe she shouldn't have come here. For the first time she began to have doubts about her own motives. Selfish, she was being selfish, and maybe she should let Ethan off the hook and tell her grandfather the truth about what had happened. It wasn't right; it wasn't

fair that Ethan should be forced to make sac-
rifices just because she'd managed to wriggle
her way beneath his tough façade and basically
run rings around him.

Is that what she'd done? Yes, it was exactly
what she'd done, she admitted. She'd wept,
she'd fought, she'd begged and had seduced
and had turned him upside down and inside
out—and all in twenty-four wild and dizzying
hours, too!

'Oh, by the way...' Victor Frayne's voice
cut through her train of thinking at about the
same moment Eve's eyes settled on a row of
framed photographs sitting on a long low cedarwood sideboard. '...the door to Leona's
bedroom is sticking. Can you get someone up
there to take a look at it?'

The call to her grandfather was forgotten. A
cold chill of dismay was settling on her skin.
Ethan couldn't—surely—have brought her to
stay at the home of Victor Frayne and Leona
Al-Qadim?

CHAPTER THIRTEEN

THE meeting had taken longer than Ethan had expected but by the end of it Ethan was satisfied that the new yacht club building was no longer under threat. As he shook hands with the local planning officials, he was aware that his site managers were standing to one side waiting to do the usual post-mortem on the meeting, but he was eager to get away.

He kept thinking of Eve and how she'd looked when he'd left her, wearing nothing but his cast-off shirt and a becoming flush to her lovely face.

As soon as the officials departed, one of his managers stepped up. 'Victor has been trying to contact you,' the man informed him. 'Something to do with Theron Herakleides and the Greek project?'

Theron, Ethan began to frown. He had forgotten all about Eve's grandfather and his threats. 'I'll deal with it.' He nodded. He glanced at his watch, realised he'd been away from Eve for over two hours, and wished he knew at what point it had been that he had become so obsessed with her that she was virtually wrapped around his every thought. 'If everything is back on track here, can we rain check the post-mortem? I need to be somewhere else.'

He was talking to all three of his site managers, and they instantly developed distinct masculine gleams in their eyes. 'We heard all about the souvenir you brought back with you from the Caribbean,' one of them teased him lazily, telling him also that the company grapevine was still working efficiently.

This kind of man-to-man camaraderie was to be expected on building sites. One either sank or swam with it. Ethan usually swam.

'The *souvenir* goes by the name of Eve Herakleides,' he informed them dryly. 'And if you value your jobs here I would suggest you curb the joky comments, because she also happens to be my future wife.'

A stunned silence fell. Ethan looked at the three men and saw their slack-jawed trance. But their shock came nowhere near the shock that he found himself experiencing. He felt as if he had just stepped off a very high cliff.

Had he really said that? Yes, he had said that, he was forced to grimly face the fact.

They were looking at him as if they expected him to laugh now and withdraw what he'd said. After all, this had to be a classic example of building-site camaraderie where the jokes flew back and forth with quick-flitting wit that did not always need to tell the truth if the punch-line served got the right results?

So—okay, this was supposed to be part of an elaborate deception, he tried to reason. But it didn't feel like a lie. Was that why he was suddenly feeling as if he'd jumped into a free fall from a fatal height?

'Nothing to say?' he mocked, working like mad to keep the jaunty flow going now that he had opened his big mouth.

'Congratulations,' one man muttered uncomfortably. The others mimicked their colleague like puppets that had just had their strings well and truly jerked.

'Thank you,' he murmured, while thinking Eve would have loved to be here to witness this. It placed the act she'd put on for her grandfather the day before yesterday right into the shade. 'Be sure to make it a good whip-round for my wedding gift when the time comes.'

They should have laughed then—told him what a fool he was for getting caught after managing to stay single for all these years. But their expressions had now shifted to something else entirely.

What else? he puzzled. What exactly was now going on inside their heads while they stood there looking at him like that?

Then it hit him. Leona. His free fall through space stopped abruptly as cold anger erupted in his breast. Did everyone in San Estéban suspect his relationship with Leona had been something other than what it was?

Now he was glad that Eve wasn't here to witness this scene, or every single suspicion she had about him and Leona would be buzzing around her possessive head.

Oh, but he liked Eve possessive; he liked her weepy and vulnerable and high-tempered and snappy; he liked her wearing hot-pink, like the dress she'd had on in the bar on the beach, and she'd had painted onto the nails she'd drawn down his chest last night.

Where the hell did he think he was going with this kind of crazy thinking? Crazy really said it. The last twenty-four hours in their entirety had been one long walk through insanity! But in those twenty-four hours, he realised he'd come to care a great deal what Eve thought about him.

'So watch the snide remarks in her presence,' he cautioned more seriously. 'She's special. I expect her to be treated as special. Make sure you pass the warning on.'

And if this performance didn't convince them that he and Leona were not an item, then what would?

'Right, Boss,' they said in solemn unison.

As he left, Ethan wondered how long it would take for this juicy snippet of information to make it right round San Estéban?

Eve was standing in the sunny lounge holding a picture frame between trembling fingers when she heard Ethan return. She was trying to decide whether to be hurt, insulted or just plain angry. She'd certainly been hurt when she'd picked up this frame, and had found herself staring at the tableau it presented of a beautiful woman standing with—not one—but *four* incredibly spectacular looking men!

One of the men was Ethan. *All* of them looked ready and willing to worship at the woman's feet. And why not? she acknowledged. The lady was really quite something special with her flowing red hair, exquisite face and the kind of smile that dropped men to their knees.

'It was taken at Leona's civil wedding in England,' Ethan's voice quietly informed her.

Looking up she saw him standing in the archway. The jacket to his suit had gone but the tie still rested neatly against his shirt front. As always, he looked heart-stoppingly attractive, even with that guarded look he was wearing on his face.

She looked away from him and back at the photograph. 'She's beautiful,' she murmured huskily.

His answering smile was more like a grimace as he walked forward to glance down at the photograph. 'Victor Frayne,' he indicated with a long finger. 'Leona, of course, and Sheikh Hassan Al-Qadim. The giant is Sheikh

Hassan's brother, Sheikh Rafiq Al-Qadim—though he refuses to acknowledge the title,' he added grimacing.

'Why?'

'Long story. Remind me to tell it to you sometime—preferably before you meet him.' Said with humour, there was nothing funny in the way he took the frame from her then stood frowning down at it before putting it back in its place.

'Is there a chance that I'll meet him?' Eve was already stiffening her insides ready for the blow she thought was coming her way. If the Al-Qadim family were here in San Estéban... If they were staying in this same house then she was...

'Not really,' he murmured. 'He goes nowhere without his brother, and his brother is cruising the Mediterranean as we speak.'

'This is their villa, isn't it?' she stated.

Did he hear the accusation in her tone? If he did, his face didn't show it as he turned with what Eve read as reluctance from the photo to look at her. 'It's the company villa,' he corrected. 'Victor designed it, Leona furnished it.

We all use it as a convenient place to live when we are here in Spain.'

Convenient, just about said it for Eve, and her mind was suddenly tripping over itself as it painted lurid pictures in her head of Ethan and Leona in their convenient love-nest with dear Papa along as one lousy chaperone!

'And where's Leona now?' she demanded.

'With her husband on their yacht. Victor flew back to London yesterday, once he knew I was coming here to take over for him.'

'So you thought, Why not bring Eve here and *conveniently* slot her in where Leona should be?'

Ethan's eyes narrowed at her waspish tone. 'What is that supposed to mean?'

'It means,' she lashed at him, 'that I do not appreciate playing substitute to anyone!'

'Substitute to who, exactly?'

He wanted her to spell it out for him. Well, she could do that! 'Leona's clothes hang in the wardrobe,' she told him. 'The next bedroom to yours as a matter of fact!'

'It bothers you?' he murmured.

'It bothers me.' She nodded. 'It more than bothers me that you dared to bring me here to your sordid little love-nest and make love to me in the same bed in which you probably made love to her!'

His grey eyes narrowed some more and Eve was suddenly thinking about dangerous animals again, and felt the fizz of excitement leap inside.

She was trembling like mad, Ethan noticed, and he was angry! 'A small piece of advice,' he offered thinly. 'Loose talk is dangerous when the Al-Qadim family is involved. So hold your foolish tongue and listen. Leona and I are not, and never have been, lovers,' he stated it with ice-cold precision. 'Take that on board and heed it, Eve, because I won't repeat it again.'

But he would say that, wouldn't he, to protect his true love? Eve had never felt so used in her entire life. 'I'm leaving,' she decided.

He didn't say anything, but just stood there looking at her through cold hard gun-metal-grey eyes.

Her heart was bursting, because she didn't really want to go. But she turned anyway and began walking towards the archway the led to the hall.

'Back to Aidan Galloway?' he fed silkily after her. 'Back to the young bloods you can handle better than you can handle me?'

She stopped. 'At least Aidan cares about my feelings.'

'By spiking your drink so he can enjoy you without needing to put much effort into it?'

She swung round. 'I told you it wasn't Aidan that did that to me!'

'Ah, yes, the other nameless young blood,' he drawled, and Eve noticed that the cynicism was back. 'Funny how you remembered him only after I threatened to tear Galloway limb from limb.'

He still didn't believe her about Aidan! she realised. 'It was Raoul Delacroix who spiked my drink!' she insisted furiously.

Raoul Delacroix. Any other name, Ethan was thinking, and he would have laughed in her lying face! But he was recalling the look on Raoul's face as he'd turned away from her in the bar at the beach. He was recalling the stinging sensation he'd experienced at the back of his neck, that reminded him he didn't like what he'd seen on the young Frenchman's face.

'And I don't know what right you think you have to throw my love life back at me when nothing could be more sordid than the set-up you have going here!'

'Leave Leona out of this,' he bit at her.

'Leave Aidan out of it!'

Stalemate. They both recognised it for what it was. She was standing there shimmering with offence and fury and he was standing there simmering in the midst of a jealous rage! He couldn't believe it. Couldn't bring himself to accept that in forty-eight short hours she could have actually brought him down to this.

'Go if you are going,' he said as the damning remark to come straight out of that last angry thought.

She turned—but not before he had seen that heart-shaped pink mouth that had a propensity to pout, quiver, and her eyes sparkle with the promise of tears. Hell, he cursed, when he knew what was going to happen: he was going to give in. He could feel it bubbling up inside him, hot and out of control.

'But—I'm coming with you.' The decision itself set his feet in motion. As he strode towards her he saw his ring sparkling on her finger when she lifted her hand up to brush a tear from her cheek.

My tears, my ring—my woman, he claimed possessively. He took all three, grabbing his woman around the waist, crushing the ring in the clasp of one of his hands, and spinning her about so that he could lick the tears from her cheek. 'Anywhere,' he murmured, while he did it. 'Hotel, an apartment in San Estéban. We can even take one of the other villas if that's what you prefer.'

Preference didn't really come into it, Eve thought helplessly. She preferred not to love him this badly. But she did. Bottom line. 'I would prefer it if Leona Al-Qadim didn't exist,' she told him honestly.

'Forget Leona,' he muttered impatiently.

'If you forget Aidan,' she returned, determined to maintain some level of balance around here.

She looked into his eyes; he looked into hers; both sets were angry because they were giving in. Their bodies liked it though, Eve noticed. They were greeting each other like hungry lovers.

'So, where are we going to go to continue this?' His voice rasped with impatience, his body pulsed with desire.

The fact that hers was doing the same thing made the decision for her. So she reached up, touched her mouth to his, and remained that close while she murmured, 'Here seems very convenient, don't you think...?'

CHAPTER FOURTEEN

THE little minx. An absolute witch, sent to torment the life out of him, Ethan was thinking irritably. There was nothing convenient about having Eve Herakleides running riot through his life.

The telephone rang. He picked it up. 'What?' he barked.

It was his secretary in London. Sitting there behind his desk, Ethan dealt with a list of queries while his angry gaze remained fixed on the little scene taking place outside his site-office window, where Eve stood laughing, surrounded by a whole rugby scrum of big, tough, very much hands-on builders wearing yellow helmets, dust-covered steel-capped boots, tight tee shirts and jeans.

And what was Eve wearing?

Hot-pink. It was her favourite colour, he had come to realise during the last ten days. Today it was hot-pink trousers that skimmed her hips and thighs and stopped just above her slender calf muscles, and a baby-pink top that left a lot of golden midriff on show.

Too much midriff. 'I don't know about that, Sonia,' he murmured. 'I can't be sure I'll be back in London to attend that meeting. You'd better ask Victor if he can do it.'

Eve's hair was up in a natty little twist that did amazing things to the length of her neck, and in profile she looked like the sweetest thing ever to be put onto this earth. Every time she moved he saw his ring flash in the sunlight. Every time she laughed he saw his men almost fall to their knees.

'I know they wanted me,' he rasped out testily. 'But they can't have me.'

I'm already engaged, he thought, to a woman with no sense of what's right or proper to wear on a building site! In the last ten days he'd also come to realise the full meaning of the term *engaged*.

'Heard anything from Theron Herakleides?' he thought to enquire.

There was another person who was irritating the hell out of him. Since their tough talk in the Caribbean, he hadn't had a single peep out of Eve's grandfather. His own letter formally withdrawing his submission for the Greek project had not been acknowledged. The promised contract making sure Ethan didn't get his greedy hands on the old man's money had never appeared. No one at Hayes-Frayne could get to speak to Herakleides, and even Leandros was complaining that the Greek had dropped off the face of the earth. As far as Ethan could make out, Theron was only answering calls from his precious granddaughter. She'd been talking to him every day, but even she couldn't get him to come clean as to what he was going to do about the Greek project. He'd just said, 'I'll see you in two weeks.' Then it had been one week. Now it was down to just a few days.

Their official betrothal. His ring on Eve's finger winked at him. 'Nothing,' he heard his secretary say.

The ring sparkled again as Eve lifted up her hand to brush some dry plaster from one man's bulging bicep. The guy grinned a very macho, very sexy, Spanish grin. Ethan felt his gut tighten up in protest. Abruptly finishing the telephone conversation, he stood up and knocked on the window-pane.

Eve turned. So did the men. She sent him a wide white brilliant smile. The men's smiles were more—manly, as in, You lucky devil, Mr Hayes.

'He wants his souvenir back,' he heard one man say to the others.

Eve laughed, as she had done from the first time she'd heard herself referred to as that. She liked it. Damn it, *he* liked it! He liked what it did to him when she sent him that teasing little smile that said, Some souvenir, hmm?

He was in love with her. He'd known it for days, weeks, maybe even months. She filled his every thought, his every sense, his every desire. He looked at her and felt a multitude of conflicting emotions, none of which on their own could adequately describe what he was having to deal with inside.

Bidding a light farewell to her macho fan club, she began walking towards his office door. He watched her come, watched her soft mouth take on a different look that was exclusively for him. It was a kiss, a sensual kiss, offered to him from a distance. She was a flirt; she was a tease; he found himself wearing an irresistible grin.

'What are you doing here?' he demanded though, the moment she came into the cool confines of his air-conditioned office. 'I thought we'd agreed you would keep away from the site so you don't cause accidents.'

She laughed; she thought he was joking, but Ethan wasn't sure that he was. Heads turned when Eve walked by. The fact that those heads were on bodies with feet balancing on ladders or on scaffolding made it dangerous.

'I needed to ask your advice about something.'

'Try the phone.'

'Oh, don't be a grouch.' She pouted up at him as she walked around his desk. Then she boldly pulled the cord that closed the sunblinds across the window and reached up to transform the pout into a kiss that wound its tentacles around him and left him wanting more.

I love this man, Eve thought, as she drew away again. I love him so much that I daren't let myself think about Athens and the fact that we have only three days to go before we are expected there.

It was frightening. She held his cheek, looked deep into his eyes and wished she knew

how much of what they relayed to her was just
sexual desire and how much was still rooted
in pretence. What she did know was that they
had been so happy here. No spats, since the
first day. No mention of anything likely to start
a war.

Except for Grandfather, of course. He was
discussed on a daily basis. But never in a way
that could remind either of them of how this
whole thing had started out.

'Was that it?' he prompted. 'You wanted my
advice on how well you kiss?'

Eve refocused her attention and saw one of
his eyebrows had arched and his mouth was
wearing a lazily amused smile. It would be the
easiest thing in the world to say yes, and leave
it at that, keep the rest until later when he came
home.

But keeping Ethan on his toes was her aim
in life. So, she said airily, 'Oh, no. I already
know what a great kisser I am.'

Stepping away from him, she applied her
surprise tactics by unzipping her trousers and
peeling them back from her hips. 'What do
you think?' she asked innocently.

Innocent was not the word Ethan was thinking as he stared down at her silk-smooth abdomen. He was thinking, Minx, again. Outrageous and unpredictable minx. For there, nestling in the hollow of her groin, just above the tantalisingly brief panty line, and right on the spot of an erogenous zone he knew so well he could actually feel its response against the flat of his tongue, lay a heart. A small red painted heart.

'It's a tattoo,' he announced.

'What do you think?' she repeated.

'I think you're not safe to be let out on your own,' he replied. 'What were you thinking of, marking your lovely skin with something like that?'

'I thought you might like it.' The pout was back, Ethan noticed, the one that begged to be soothed into something else.

Well, not this time. 'You idiot,' he snapped. 'That's going to hurt like blazes by tonight.'

'No, it won't,' she denied. 'Because it isn't real. I found this amazing little shop down one of the back streets in San Estéban where they apply these temporary tattoos. It will disappear in about a month. I think its great.' Eve looked down to view her latest impulse. 'I might have it replaced with a permanent one next time.'

'Over my dead body,' he vowed, but he had to reach out to run his thumb pad over the painted heart. As he did so he heard her breath quiver in her throat and felt the sound replay itself in other parts of himself.

He knew that sound. He looked at her face and saw her innocent green eyes had darkened into those of an outright sinner. His body quickened; she saw it happen; her mouth stretched into a knowing smile. 'It will be interesting to see if you change your mind about that,' she taunted silkily.

It was no use, Ethan gave up—as he always seemed to do. Swinging his chair around, he sat himself down then drew her in between his spread thighs. 'No,' he refused, knowing exactly what she believed was going to come. Instead he tugged the zip shut on her trousers, then took a firm grip on both of her hips and brought her tumbling down on his lap. Kisses on the mouth were much less evocative than kisses elsewhere. This way at least he would manage to hang onto some of his dignity if anyone should happen to walk in here.

By the time the kissing stopped, her eyes were glazed—but then so were his. 'I'm going to send you packing now,' he told her huskily.

'But you would rather come with me.'

It was no lie. 'If that tattoo hurts later, we are going to have a row,' he warned.

'It won't,' she stated confidently.

The telephone on his desk began to ring. Maybe it was good timing on its part because it put a stop to what was still promising to develop into something else.

'Up,' he commanded, and used his hands to set her back on her feet, then urged her towards the door. 'Now go and don't come back.' On that brisk dismissal he reached out for the phone. 'And leave my labourers alone!' he added as she was about to walk out of the door.

She turned, sent him a look that stirred his blood. Then she caught him off guard, yet again. 'I did it for you, you know,' she softly confided. 'You're going to love it, I promise you.'

'Ethan Hayes,' he announced into the telephone, as he stood up to open the blinds so he could watch Eve walk towards the car he had hired for her to use.

The whole site had come to a stop. He watched it happen, watched her take no notice of any of the remarks that flew her way. He also saw her pause, look back and wave to let him know that she knew he was watching her. By the time she'd turned away again he knew that his own departure wasn't going to be that far away.

He was right, but for the wrong reasons. 'Ethan—' it was Victor '—you are not going to like this, but I need to ask you to do me a very big favour…'

Eve had been back at the villa for less than half an hour when she heard Ethan come in through the door. Not expecting him for hours yet—even with the invitation she had left behind her earlier—she had just curled up in a shady spot on the terrace with the book her grandfather had given her for her birthday. It was a rare first edition of classical Greek love poems to add to the collection he had been building for her since her first birthday.

But the moment she heard Ethan's step, the book was forgotten, a look of surprised delight already lighting her face at this major triumph in managing to get him to come back early because he couldn't resist the invitation she'd so blatantly left him with.

'I'm on the terrace!' she called out and un-curled her feet from beneath her then stood up to go and meet him halfway. She reached the door through to the sitting room as he appeared in the arch leading into it from the hall. He stopped, she stopped. It took less than a second to make her welcoming smile fade from her face when she saw the expression on his. It was like being tossed back eleven days to that bar on the Caribbean beach, he looked so different.

CHAPTER FIFTEEN

'WHAT'S wrong?' she asked sharply, absolutely sure that something had to be, because no man changed so very much in such a short space of time without having a reason for doing so.

He didn't reply, not immediately anyway. Instead he built the tension by grimly yanking the tie loose from his collar and tossing it aside then releasing his top shirt-button before issuing a heavy sigh.

'We need to talk,' he said on the back of that sigh. That was all, no warm greeting, no teasing comment about the little red heart she was wearing for him.

Fear began to walk all over her self-confidence, 'W-what about?'

'You and me,' he replied, ran a hand round the back of his neck as if to attempt to ease the tension she could see he was suffering from. 'We've been living a lie for the last ten days, Eve. Have you ever stopped to think about that?'

Think about it? She lived with it! Ate, slept and made love to it!

'For me it stopped being a lie from the first time we made love, Ethan,' she answered. 'So maybe you had better tell me whether you've thought about it much recently.'

Her sarcasm hit a nerve, but instead of an answer he made a grimace that she just did not like. Something had happened; it had to have done to change the man she had left only an hour ago into this person who was so uptight she could actually feel his tension cutting through the air like a sharp knife. And worse: he had stopped looking at her.

'I have to go away for a few days,' he suddenly announced.

That was the root of all of this tension? 'Well, that's all right,' she murmured, unable to believe that was the answer to what was bothering him. Forcing herself to walk forwards on legs that weren't all that steady, she tried to look calm as she placed her book down on a nearby table then turned to look expectantly at him. 'Business?' she asked.

'Yes—no.' He changed his mind and began to frown. 'It's more an errand of mercy...' Then he muttered, 'Damn this, Eve—I'm trying to find out if you intend to still be here when I get back.'

Was that all? Staring at him, Eve couldn't believe the sense of relief that went flooding through her. 'Of course!' she exclaimed. 'Why ever not?'

For some bewildering reason, her reply only filled him with exasperation and he strode forward to grasp her left hand then lifted it up to her face. 'Because this ring,' he uttered tightly, 'will become a formal engagement ring on Saturday in Athens. So if you want out, you have to say so now.'

'Do you want out?'

'No.' He sighed. 'I do not want out. I just needed to know where I stand with you before I—'

'Well, I don't want out,' she cut in softly, and her smile came back to her eyes, to her slightly quivering mouth. 'I want you.'

He loved that mouth, Ethan reaffirmed something he already knew. He loved this woman. But was her 'I want you' enough to make him declare himself?

Was it enough to get him through the rest of what he had to tell her. 'Enough to trust me?' he therefore had to ask.

'Trust you about what?'

Well, here it comes, he thought, the bottom line to all of this. He took a deep breath, let it out again, desperately wanted to kiss her first, but held back on the need and looked deep into her beautiful green eyes. 'Victor Frayne called me as you were leaving the office. He needs a very big favour from me. Due to unfounded rumours involving me and his daughter Leona, her marriage is under threat. So I am flying out to Rahman to help scotch those rumours—at her husband Sheikh Hassan's request.'

He added Hassan's name to give it all sanction. He hoped it would hold a lot of sway. But silence came back at him, though it wasn't really silence because Eve's eyes told him a lot; their warm green slowly froze over until they'd turned to arctic frost. Her kissable mouth became a hard cold untouchable line, and loudest of all, she snatched her hand out of his and curled it into a tight fist at her side.

'You're still in love with her, you bastard,' she whispered.

'No.' He denied it. 'Leona needs—'

'To know she still has you dangling on a string.'

Coming from the very woman who had him dangling, Ethan couldn't help but laugh at that.

Eve's response was to step around him and walk coldly away.

She had never felt so betrayed. He'd manoeuvred that discussion, worked it and her like a master conductor until he'd got her to say what he'd wanted to hear, before he'd told her what he'd known she had not wanted to hear.

And for what purpose? Had he received a telephone call from her grandfather also? Did he now know, as she did, that the Greek project was about to be awarded to Hayes-Frayne?

'Don't do this, Eve,' he threaded heavily after her.

She didn't want to listen—refused to listen, and just kept on walking out of the sitting room and down the hall into the bedroom. *Their* bedroom. The one they'd been sharing since the first night he'd brought her here. She hated him for that. She now hated him so very badly that she could barely draw breath over that burgeoning hate.

He arrived in the doorway just as she was flipping her case open on the bed. A sense of *déjà vu* washed over her; only, last time this scene had been played their roles had been reversed.

'Eve—this is important.' He tried an appeal.

She almost laughed at his choice of words, coming hard on the back of what she had just been likening this moment to.

'We are talking about an Arab state here— a Muslim state where women are held sacrosanct. The smallest hint of a scandal and she can be cast out into the wilderness without a single qualm. I have to go.'

'I'm not stopping you,' she pointed out.

'This is stopping me!' he rasped back angrily.

'Okay.' She turned on him in the midst of her own sudden fury. 'You don't go and I don't go!'

It was the gauntlet tossed down on the tiles between them. Ethan even looked down as if he could see it lying there—while Eve held her breath, though it didn't stop her heart from thundering madly in her ears, or fine tremors from attacking her flesh.

Because this was do or die. He chose her over Leona or it was finished for them. He knew that, she knew that.

His eyes lifted slowly, dark lashes uncurling to reveal stone-cold reservoirs of determined grey. 'The rumours are lies,' he stated. 'Just a cruel and ruthless pack of lies put about by Sheikh Hassan's enemies with the deliberate intention of forcing him to reject his wife and take another one. His father is dying. A power struggle is on. Leona is caught right in the middle because she cannot bear his child. Those who don't want to unseat Hassan from power are pressurising him to take a second wife who can give him that child. If you have one small portion of understanding what that must be like for her, then you will accept that I cannot turn my back on her need for my support now.'

'How does your going to Rahman scotch those rumours?' Eve questioned with an icy scepticism that made him release a short tight laugh.

'If you knew the ways of Arab politics you would know that no Arab would invite his wife's lover into his house,' he explained. 'I am to be placed on show.' The laughter died. 'Held up in front of Rahman's best and most powerful as a man Hassan trusts and admires. And if you think I'm looking forward to that, then you're wrong,' he grimly declared.

'So you love her enough to put her needs before your own pride,' Eve concluded. And that was what this was really all about. Not whether he went or whether he stayed. It was about whether he still loved Leona enough to do it. The rest was just icing to cover an ugly cake.

'I'm going home, to Athens,' she told him flatly. 'This is it. We are finished.'

Ethan released another very bitter laugh. 'Well,' he said, 'at least you managed to do what you set out to do. You gave yourself two weeks to get around to jilting me. You're even slightly ahead of time. Well done, Eve.'

With that, it was Ethan who walked away.

Why? Because he had his answer. If she'd loved him, she would have trusted him. If she'd cared about anyone but herself, she would have understood why he had to go.

Funny really, he thought, when only five minutes later he walked out of the villa and climbed into his car. A bit of encouragement on Eve's part and he would probably have invited her to go to Rahman with him. She would have enjoyed the novelty of watching him be foisted up as a pillar of good old-fashioned gentlemanly honour, when she knew the real man could take a sweet virgin and turn her into a sex goddess.

Too late now. He didn't want a woman that couldn't trust his word, and she didn't want a man who didn't jump to her bidding every time she told him to. On that most final of thoughts on the subject of Eve Herakleides, he started the car and drove out of the courtyard then turned to skirt San Estéban so he could meet the main road to Malaga.

While Eve still stood where he had left her, staring at nothing, feeling nothing—was too scared to feel.

The sound of the front door closing only five minutes later came as a big shock though. She hadn't expected him to leave so soon. She hadn't realised the end was going to be so quick and so cold.

She even shivered, found herself staring at Tigger who was sitting where he always sat, on the table beside the bed. He was looking at her as if to ask what kind of fool she was.

Well, she knew she was a fool. She'd worked so very hard to bring Ethan to the point where he'd want her to keep his ring on her finger. Now she'd thrown it all away.

Was that good or bad? Staring down at the ring, she watched its sparkle grow dim behind a bank of tears, and knew her failure was not in making Ethan want her, but in failing to make him love her.

Malaga airport was packed as always. Ethan arrived just in time to catch his flight to London, where he would have time only to go to his apartment, catch a couple of hours' sleep then pack a bag before he was due to link up with Victor for their trip to Rahman.

Eve took the easier option, and rang her cousin Leandros to beg the use of his helicopter to take her to Malaga. Therefore she arrived long before Ethan got there, and had taken off for Athens by the time he pulled his car into a long-stay slot.

London was cold. He didn't mind; the heavy grey skies suited his mood. It wasn't until he thought to check his emails before shooting off to meet Victor, that he found a note from his secretary telling him that Theron Herakleides had come out of hiding and was now making hopeful murmurings about Hayes-Frayne being awarded the Greek project.

'Well, shoot that in the foot,' he told the computer screen, and switched it off. As of now, Hayes-Frayne could kiss goodbye anything to do with Greece.

He wished he'd kissed Eve goodbye before he'd left...

Athens was hot, stifling beneath one of its famous heatwaves. Eve was glad to let the taxi cab drive her up into the hills where the air was more fit to breathe. Her grandfather's mansion house stood in a row of gracious old houses occupying one of the most prestigious plots the rambling city had to offer.

He was just sitting down to dinner when she walked in, unannounced. 'My angel!' he greeted in surprise, and got to his feet to come down the table for his expected embrace.

He was not expecting her to burst into a flood of tears though. 'Oh, Grandpa!' She sobbed as she walked into his arms. 'I hate him. I hate him so much!'

CHAPTER SIXTEEN

THE palace of Al-Qadim made an impressive sight standing against a backcloth of a star-studded night sky. Its rich sandstone walls had been flood-lit from below and, as they drove through the arched gateway into its huge inner courtyard, Ethan was reluctantly impressed with the sheer scale and beauty that met his eyes.

But he didn't want to be here. He was angry and fed up with role-playing for other people's benefit. He was sick to his stomach with the Mr Honourable tab people seemed to like to stick on him. The Mr you-can-depend-on-me-to-bale-you-out label.

He grimaced. Somewhere back there across a large tract of land and an ocean, he was being summarily sacked from his latest role with the none too tasty word *jilted* to wear as an epitaph to that little affair. While here, he was about to become the focus of critical Arab eyes, when he received his second sacking in twenty-four hours from the role as wicked lover to the Sheikha Leona Al-Qadim.

'Ethan—if you don't want to go ahead with this, then say so,' Victor murmured beside him.

'I'm here, aren't I?' he answered tersely, but then his whole manner had been terse since he'd climbed into his car in Spain and had driven away from Eve.

Eve the flirt, Eve the temptress, Eve the serpent, who'd made the last two weeks a perfect paradise—before she'd reverted to her original form. And what was that? he asked himself. Eve, the spoiled little rich girl, who wanted everything to go her way.

He was best out of it. He should have known that before it began. He should have seen the idiot he was making of himself every time he let her weave her magic spells around him.

The trouble was, he'd liked it. He'd liked playing slave to Eve Herakleides and her whims. She turned him on, hard and fast. She made him feel alive.

She'd had a heart temporarily tattooed onto one of her most erogenous spots just to tease him out of his mind.

'Only, in this mood, you aren't what I would call sociable,' Victor inserted carefully.

'Watch me turn on when the curtain goes up,' he promised. 'I'll be so sociable with your son-in-law that they will start to wonder if it's Hassan I've been having the affair with.'

'Don't be facetious.'

Victor was getting angry. Ethan didn't particularly blame him.

'You should have brought her with you if you can't last a day out of her arms without turning into a grouch.'

'Who are we talking about?' Ethan's eyes flashed a warning glance at the other man.

Victor just smiled one of those smiles that people smiled around him these days. 'I might not have been to San Estéban recently, but even the London-office cleaner knows about the *souvenir* you brought back from the Caribbean.'

Souvenir from hell, he amended bitterly.

Then he saw her expression just before he'd turned his back on her for the last time, and his insides knotted into a tight ball. He'd hurt her with all of this. He'd known that he would. That's why he'd tried to find out where she'd wanted their relationship to go, before he'd told her about this trip.

He'd wanted her to understand. He'd wanted her to trust him. See, for goodness' sake, that he couldn't be in love with another woman when she possessed every single inch of him!

So—what now? What was he doing here? A sudden and uncontrollable aching tension attached itself to his bones. He should be back there, arguing with Eve, not snapping at Victor! She was right in a lot of ways: he should have put her feelings first!

Oh, hell, damn it, he cursed.

The car came to stop in front of a beautiful lapis-lazuli-lined dome suspended between pillars made of white marble. Beyond the dome he could see a vast entrance foyer glittering beneath Venetian crystal. Victor got out of the car. Ethan did the same. As they stepped towards the dome, he shrugged his wide shoulders and grimly swapped Eve-tension for play-your-part-tension—so he could get the hell out of here.

Dressed in black western dinner suites, white shirts and bow ties, he and Victor stood out in a room filled with flowing Arabian colour. He saw Leona straight away. She was wearing gold-threaded blood-red silk and she looked absolutely radiant. Beside her stood the man she had adored from the first moment she'd set eyes on him just over five years ago, Sheikh Hassan Al-Qadim—who looked unusually pale for a man of his rich colouring.

Had the strain of the last few weeks begun to get to him? Victor had relayed some of what had been going on. Hassan had been fighting the battle of his life to keep the wife of his choice by his side *and* retain his place as his father's successor as ruler of Rahman. He had achieved success on both fronts—by the skin of his teeth.

Other than for this one last thing...

The hairs on the back of Ethan's neck began to prickle. A brief, smooth scan of the room showed him what he had expected to see. People were staring at him—in shock, in dismay, in avid curiosity.

Were they expecting a scene? Were they looking like that because they expected Hassan to call for his sword and have his head taken off?

The prickle at the back of his neck increased, when what had been meant as a bit of sardonic whimsy suddenly didn't seem that whimsical at all. Then common sense returned, because what use would it be to have his head severed from his shoulders when all that would do would be to prove that Hassan believed the rumours about his beautiful wife?

What he was doing was far more subtle. The man had style, Ethan was prepared to acknowledge when, on catching sight of him standing here next to Victor, Hassan did not reveal a hint of the old dislike that usually flashed between the two of them. Instead Ethan saw him smile, then gently touch Leona's arm to draw her attention their way.

Leona turned to towards them. By now the room was held enthralled. Her lovely face began to lighten. A pair of stunning green eyes, that somehow were not quite as stunning to him as another pair of green eyes, flicked from her father's face to his face then quickly back again. Then, on a small shriek of delight, she launched herself towards them.

It seemed as if the whole assembly took a step backwards in shocked readiness for her to reveal her true feelings for this western man. Tall, lean and in very good shape for his fifty-five years, Victor Frayne received his daughter into his arms and accepted her ecstatic kisses to his face while Ethan felt the room almost sag in relief, or disappointment, depending on whether they were friend or foe to Sheikh Hassan Al-Qadim.

'What are you doing here? Why didn't you tell me?' Leona was scolding her father through a bank of delighted tears.

'Ethan—' She turned those starry eyes on him next and reached out to capture his hand. 'I can't believe this! I thought you were in San Estéban!'

'I only spoke to you this morning in London.' She was talking to her father again.

'No, a hotel, here.' Her father grinned at her. 'Thank your husband for the surprise.'

Hassan appeared at Leona's side to lay a hand on her slender waist. Leona turned those shining eyes onto him. 'I love you,' she murmured impulsively.

'She desires to make me blush,' Hassan said dryly, then offered his hand first to his father-in-law then to Ethan. 'Glad you could make it,' he said congenially. 'We are honoured to receive you into our home.'

'The honour is all mine,' Ethan replied with a smile that held only a touch of irony to imply that there was more to this invitation than met the eye.

Hassan sent him a slight grimace, then looked down at Leona who was too excited to notice any of the undercurrents flowing around her.

She didn't know, Ethan realised. She had no idea that he was here to help save her reputation. His estimation of Sheikh Hassan rose a couple of notches in recognition of the lengths he was prepared to go to for his love of Leona.

Could he have ever loved her like that? Looking at her laughing, beautiful face, he found himself superimposing another laughing, beautiful face over the top of it, and had to ask himself if he'd ever loved Leona at all? For this other face didn't just laugh at him, it teased and flirted and sent him secret little come-and-get-me smiles that made his insides sing. This other face looked at him and loved him.

Loved him? He stopped to question that.

Loved him, he repeated. His legs almost went from under him as his heart sank like a stone.

It was there, he could see it. It was there. He'd been blind!

'Ethan, are you feeling okay?'

He blinked and found himself looking down at Leona's anxious face. 'Fine.' He smiled. 'I'm glad to see you looking so happy.'

Stupidly, utterly, totally blind!

'I am!' She smiled. 'Deliriously happy.'

I need to get out of here...

'Good,' he said. 'This time make sure you hang onto it.'

In solemn response, she linked her arm with Hassan's arm. 'Hanging on,' she softly promised him.

He was supposed to laugh so he did laugh. Half the room turned to stare at the two of them and because Hassan must have seen all his hard work going down the tubes, he suddenly laughed as well and so did Victor.

As if cued by this brief moment of danger, another diversion was suddenly grabbing everyone's attention. People stopped talking. Silence rained down on the whole assembly as

Hassan's half-brother, Rafiq, appeared pushing a wheelchair bearing Sheikh Khalifa ben Jusef Al-Qadim.

Ethan had only met the elderly sheikh once before, five years ago at his son's wedding. But he still couldn't believe the changes wrought since then. The old man looked so thin and frail against the height and breadth of his youngest son—a wasted shadow of his former self. But his eyes were bright, his mouth smiling and, in the frozen stasis brought on by everyone's shock at how ill he actually looked, he was prepared, and ready to respond. 'Welcome—welcome everyone,' he greeted. 'Please, do not continue to look at me as if you are attending my wake, for I assure you I am here to enjoy myself.'

After that everyone made themselves relax again. Some who knew him well even grinned. As Rafiq wheeled him towards the other end of the room, the old Sheikh missed no one in reach of his acknowledgement. 'Victor,' he greeted. 'I have stolen your daughter. She is now my most precious daughter, I apologise to you, but am not sorry, you understand.'

'I think we can share her,' Victor Frayne replied smilingly.

'And...ah.' The old sheikh then turned to Ethan. 'Mr Hayes, it is my great pleasure to meet Leona's very good friend.'

He had the floor, as it should be, so no one could miss the message being broadcast. 'Victor...Mr Hayes...come and see me tomorrow. I have a project I believe will be of great interest to you... Ah, Rafiq, take me forward for I can see Sheikh Raschid...'

And there it was, Ethan saw. In a simple exchange of pleasantries, the rumours had been scotched, dismissed and forgotten, because there wasn't a person here who would continue to question Leona's fidelity after Sheikh Khalifa himself had made his own opinions so very clear.

The old sheikh moved on, the spotlight shifted. For the next couple of hours, Hassan consolidated on what his father had put into place by taking Ethan and Victor with him around the room and introducing them to some very influential people.

I'm going crazy, Ethan decided. Because here I am smiling and talking to a lot of people

I don't even care about, when I could be some-where else with someone I do care about.

And where was Eve? Was she still at the villa in San Estéban, or had she made good her word and gone back to Athens? He wanted to know. He needed to know. His mobile phone began to burn a hole in his pocket.

In the end he couldn't stand it. He left the throng and went outside to see if he could get a signal. It wasn't a problem, so he stabbed the quick-dial button that would connect him to the villa, then stood breathing in the jasmine-scented night air while he waited to discover what his fate was going to be. What he got was the answering machine, which told him exactly nothing.

Frustration began to war with tension in his breast. Someone came to stand beside him. It was Hassan, looking less the arrogant bastard that he'd always seen him to be.

'Thank you,' Hassan said. 'I owe you a great debt of gratitude for coming here like this.'

Where it came from, Ethan had no idea, but he was suddenly so desperate to be somewhere else entirely that he knew he couldn't stay here a single moment longer. 'Do you think that debt of gratitude could stretch to a quick exit from here?' he asked curtly.

Hassan stiffened. 'You dislike our hospitality?'

'No.' He laughed. Only, it wasn't a real laugh because it erred too close to the threshold of panic. 'I just need to be somewhere else.'

She was calling him. Like the witch she was, she was casting a spell somewhere, he was sure of it. He could feel her tugging him back to her like a dog on a lead. And he wanted to go back. He didn't even mind the lead he could feel tightening around his neck. He wanted his woman. He *needed* his woman.

Maybe he knew. Maybe Sheikh Hassan Al-Qadim wasn't all self-centred arrogance. Because he simply glanced at him, just glanced, once, read something in his face—heartache, heartbreak, heart-something anyway—and with a click of his fingers he brought a servant running.

'Have my plane made ready for an immediate departure,' he instructed smoothly. 'Mr Hayes, your transport to…somewhere… awaits,' he then drawled sardonically.

CHAPTER SEVENTEEN

EVE was casting spells in the garden. They wound around a tall, dark, idiot Englishman with no heart worth mentioning.

She wasn't happy. Everyone in her grandfather's house knew that she wasn't happy. She'd rowed with Grandpa. No one had ever heard Eve row with her grandpa.

But, like the Englishman, she had come to realise that Theron Herakleides had no heart either. He'd let her down. When she'd needed his comfort and support more than she'd ever needed it, he had withdrawn both with an abruptness that shocked.

'No, Eve,' he said. 'I will not let you do this.'

'But you don't have a say in the matter!' she cried.

'On this point I do,' he insisted. 'I gave you two weeks to come to your senses about that man. When you did nothing but claim how much you adored him, I gave in to your wishes, soft-hearted fool that I am, and went ahead with planning tonight's party. You are not, therefore, going to make the Herakleides name look foolish, by cancelling at this late juncture!'

'But I no longer have a man to become betrothed to!'

'Then find one,' he advised. 'Or you will dance alone tonight, my precious,' Theron coolly informed her, 'with your honour lying on the floor by your pretty feet and the Herakleides pride lying beside it.'

'You don't mean it,' she denounced.

But he did mean it. Which was why she was sitting in the garden wondering what she was supposed to do about a party she didn't want, meant to celebrate a betrothal she didn't want, to a man who wasn't here to share either even if she did want him!

Where was he?

Her heart gave a little whimper. Was he with Leona right now, worshipping the unattainable, while her long-suffering husband played the grim chaperone—just to save face?

I hope they've had him thrown into a dungeon, she decided savagely. I hope they've cast him out into the desert with no food and water and definitely no tent!

But *where* was he? her stupid heart cried.

Today was Saturday. Yesterday she'd left a message on the answering machine in San Estéban asking him to call her. Couldn't he have done that at least? He owed her that one small consideration for all the love she'd poured into him.

I want him back. I *don't* want him back. She stood up, sat down again, let her hands wring together, looked down to find the thumb from the right hand rubbing anxiously at a finger on the left where Ethan's ring used to be.

I miss it. I miss him. Come and get me, Ethan! Oh, good grief, she never knew anything could feel this wretched.

'Eve...'

'Go away, Grandpa.' She didn't want to speak to anyone.

'There was a telephone call for you—'

'From Ethan—?' She shot eagerly back to her feet. Seeing the pity in her grandfather's eyes made her wish the ground would open up and swallow her whole.

What have I let that man do to me?

'It was Aidan Galloway,' her grandpa told her. 'He is on his way from the airport. I said you would be glad to see him.'

'Why?' Her green eyes began to spark with aggression. 'Are you thinking that Aidan could stand in as substitute?'

It made her even angrier when he dared to laugh. 'That is not a bad idea, sweetness,' he mused lazily. 'He will be here in a few minutes. I will leave you to put the suggestion to him.' With that he strolled off, still grinning from ear to ear.

He was enjoying this, Eve realised. It amazed her that she hadn't realised before what a twisted sense of humour her grandfather possessed. Her life was on the line here— her one hope at happiness—and he thought it was funny to watch her tear herself apart?

Theron did pause for a moment to wonder whether he should put her out of her misery and tell her what he already knew. He had been in touch with Victor Frayne about the Greek project. Victor Frayne had, in turn, told him about Ethan's quick departure from Rahman.

If the man wasn't coming to claim his granddaughter, then his name wasn't Theron Herakleides. Keeping Eve unaware of this prediction was good for her character. Good things came too easily for Eve, he'd come to realise. She had sailed through her life without feeling the pangs that hunger breeds. She had wit, she had grace, she had charm and intelligence, and she knew how to use them all to reach her goals with ease. But love stood on its own as something that must be worked at if it was to develop into its fullest potential. Feeling the sharp-edged fear of losing love should make her appreciate and heed the fear of losing it again.

Why did he feel she needed to do that? Because Ethan Hayes was a man of hidden fibre, he'd discovered. To keep up with the sneaky devil she was going to have to learn dexterity and speed.

Ethan landed in Athens and had to utilise some dexterity and speed to get through an airport that the rest of the world had seemed to decide to use at the same time.

He managed to grab a taxi by jumping the queue with the help of a British fifty-pound note. The drive through the city set his teeth on edge. The heat, the crowded streets, the knowledge that he had taken a chance and come here directly from Rahman, instead of checking out San Estéban, all helping to play on his stress levels. So, by the time he passed through the gates of the Herakleides mansion, he was beginning to regret this madly impulsive decision to chase after Eve.

The taxi pulled to a halt in front of a stone-fronted residence built to emulate Greek classicism at its most grand. A maid opened the door to him, smiled in recognition of the times he had been here before. When he asked to see Eve, she offered to take his suit bag from him then directed him towards the garden at the rear of the house.

His heart began to pump with the adrenaline rush of relief because he now knew his instincts had not let him down and he had been right to miss out San Estéban to come straight here.

It was mid-afternoon and as he stepped out onto the wide stone-flagged terrace the air was just taking on the warm golden glow that reminded him of the Caribbean. Striding forward he paused at the head of a set of wide shallow steps which led down into the garden. Standing on a hill as the house did, the garden itself sloped away from him in a riot of summer colour, so from up here he should easily be able to pick out Eve.

He did so immediately. It would have been impossible not to do when she was wearing a hot-pink stretchy top with a short lavender skirt. She stood out in this garden of colour like the most exotic flower ever created. As his heart began to pound in response to wrapping all of that vivid colour to him and never letting go of it again, he saw her move, realised that she wasn't alone, realised that she was also standing in the exact same spot he had seen her standing the last time he'd seen her here— and locked in the arms of the same man.

Aidan Galloway—she was locked in the arms of Aidan Galloway! Lightning was striking twice again, using a burning blast of cynical reality to hit him full in the face.

Aidan Galloway. It was a joke. He almost laughed. Only he didn't feel like laughing. Turn, he told himself. Leave, he told himself. Get away from here before she sees you and knows what a bloody fool you've made of yourself.

'Oh, Aidan,' Eve sobbed into his shoulder. 'I've made such a fool of myself!'

'Join the club,' Aidan said.

'He isn't going to come, and I've left this stupid message on his machine...'

'Now it's playing over and over in your head. I know.' Aidan sighed. 'Been there, done that, felt the agony.'

'I hate Ethan Hayes.' She sobbed into his shoulder.

'I wish I could learn to hate Corin,' Aidan murmured wistfully.

'Oh.' Eve touched his cheek. 'Is she still—?'

'Yes.'

Eve playing Eve, Ethan observed bitterly, as he watched her lift up her head and gaze into Galloway's eyes.

He felt his muscles go into violent spasm, as a need to go down there and commit murder swelled in his chest. He was about to take his first step towards assuaging that desire when a hand touched him on the shoulder, making him spin round and almost explode all that violence on Theron Herakleides instead.

'Come back inside, Mr Hayes,' Eve's grandfather said quietly.

'That's Aidan Galloway she's with,' he heard himself murmur hoarsely.

'Yes, I know it is.' Theron's steely head nodded. 'But angry men do not confront weaker men. So come inside,' he repeated the invitation. 'I have a matter I would like to discuss with you.'

Business, Ethan surmised, and shrugged the older man's hand from his shoulder. 'Keep your business proposals for someone else,' he said. He had taken enough from other people trying to direct his life. 'I'm leaving.' And he turned to stride back into the house.

Theron followed. 'Take care, Mr Hayes, what you say right now,' he quietly advised. 'For a man can still be chased through the courts here in Greece, for jilting his betrothed...'

There were several words used in that comment that stirred Ethan's blood. Jilting, was one of them, he chose to challenge another one. 'There was no betrothal,' he coldly denied. It was all just an elaborate sham thought up by the manipulating witch wearing hot-pink.

'How many witnesses do you think will I find in San Estéban who would be willing to swear the opposite to that?'

Ethan stopped walking, turned and looked at Eve's grandfather, aware that there was still more to come.

'Ah,' Theron said. 'I see you understand me. Then we will go in here and continue to discuss the small matter of a settlement...'

With that, Theron opened the door to his study and walked inside. After a small hesitation, Ethan followed him with the word settlement ringing warning bells in his head.

Theron's study was furnished to suit the man's big persona. Heavy furniture filled the floor space, heavy-framed portraits adorned the walls.

'So,' the big man began as he slotted himself behind his heavy oak desk. 'Did you really think that you could send my granddaughter back to me like used and broken goods without paying a heavy price?'

Broken. That word made Ethan release a hard mocking laugh. There had been nothing broken about the woman he'd seen wrapped in the arms of another man. 'Ask Aidan Galloway to pay the price,' he suggested. 'He has the money. You'll struggle to get a penny out of me.'

'Eve loves you.'

'Hell, damn it!' Ethan suddenly exploded spectacularly. 'Open your eyes, Theron! Eve only loves the thrill of the chase!'

Through the fine silk drapes covering the opened French window of her grandfather's study, Eve heard the deep rasping tones of Ethan's voice, froze for a split second, then spun around to stare at the house.

'Be assured that Aidan Galloway is more than willing to take your place tonight,' Theron smoothly replied. 'Oh, yes,' he confirmed at Ethan's sudden stillness. 'Eve's betrothal celebration will take place tonight whether or not it is you standing at her side. Eve is resigned to this. You've broken her heart, now she cares not about the man who will next share her bed.'

The words were used as well-aimed bullets that sank themselves deep into Ethan's head. Was that what Eve was doing out there—seducing Aidan Galloway to take his place? More bells began ringing, a red tide of anger came flooding in. He was very intimate with Eve's powers of persuasion. He knew only too well what it was like to fall into her sticky web.

'What do you want from me, Theron?' he demanded grimly.

'I want you to honour those promises you made to me in the Caribbean,' the big man said.

'I'll talk to her.' It was Ethan's only concession, though he was planning to do a lot more than just talk to Eve when he could get his hands on her. She played with men's feelings. She walked all over their self-respect. She made love like a natural-born seducer and he was damned if any other man was going to know how good that felt.

'Not without the right,' Theron smoothly said.

Ethan glared at him. 'Explain,' he insisted.

Theron went one better and slid several documents across the top of his desk. 'You know the score. Sign, and you can talk to my granddaughter. Don't sign, and you can leave her to Aidan Galloway's adequate care.'

Ah, Ethan thought. The contract to protect Theron's precious money. He almost laughed in the old man's face as he stepped up to the desk, picked up Theron's handy pen, and scrawled his signature in the allotted space.

'Now, if you will excuse me,' he concluded coldly.

'Don't you think you should have read what it is you've just put your signature to? It is an unwise man who signs a document without first ensuring himself that he has not just signed his entire wealth away.'

Wealth, Ethan thought. 'What wealth?' he mocked. His wealth stood outside in the arms of another man.

His wealth, his woman—hell, he was right back on track again; he felt so much better for realising that.

'You're a liar, Hayes,' Theron inserted, then suddenly let rip with a hearty laugh. 'Do you think I would let you seduce my granddaughter into marriage without having you thoroughly checked out? You are a Caledonian Hayes of the merchant shipping line. Your grandfather sold up in the sixties and died in the eighties, leaving you so much money you could even afford to buy me out!'

'Ah—my credentials,' Ethan acknowledged and the depth of his cynicism played havoc with his face. 'How long have you been planning this?' he demanded.

'Marrying you to my granddaughter? Two weeks ago you became worthy of consideration when my nephew, Leandros, let slip how much money you had invested in San Estéban,' Theron replied. 'A mere architect, no matter how gifted he is, could not earn that kind of money in a hundred years. I have an instinct for these things.' With a smugness that said he was enjoying himself, Theron touched a finger to the end of his nose. 'The nose twitched. So I decided to have you checked out for curiosity sake, you understand. And for Eve's sake, of course.'

Glancing down at the document he had just put his signature to, Ethan began to wonder what he had signed away. 'It won't do you any

good,' he announced. 'I live off my earned in-
come. Any money my grandfather left me is
tied up in trusts for any children I might have.'

'Or my grandchildren.' Theron nodded. 'Exactly.'

So that was what this was all about. 'Eve is
up for sale to the man with the biggest return.'

From sitting there wallowing in his own
self-satisfied smugness, Theron was suddenly
launching to his feet in a towering rage. 'Don't
speak about Eve in that tone!' he bellowed. 'It
is okay for you with your hidden millions to
stand here mocking me whose wealth is well
documented. But place yourself in Eve's shoes
and tell me how *she* distinguishes between the
man who will love her for herself and the one
with love only for the money she will inherit
one day!'

'So you think that by finding her a husband
who is wealthier than herself, you are safe-
guarding her against disillusionment and a broken heart?' Ethan's tone poured contempt all
over that concept as his own fury rose to match
the older man's. 'Money in the bank is no
guarantee for love, Theron!' he bit out furiously. 'It's just—money in the bank! I am as

capable as the next man is of breaking her foolish, reckless heart!'

'If you were the kind of man to do that, you would not be standing here arguing with me about this!'

'She already thinks I'm in love with another woman!' he threw at Theron. 'Are you telling me that your investigation of me did not tell you that?'

'If it didn't, he knows now,' another quieter, heart-piercingly level voice inserted.

CHAPTER EIGHTEEN

BOTH men stiffened sharply, both turned to stare at the silk-draped window where Eve now stood. Both men went as pale as death.

'Eve, that wasn't said to—'

The flick of a hand silenced him; the expression on her face tore him apart. She was hurting, he was hurting. Ethan didn't even want to know what Theron was feeling like. Big, green how-could-you-both-hurt-me-like-this eyes flicked from one man to the other. She took in a breath of air. It seemed to pull all of the oxygen out of the room and left none for them to breathe.

Pale but composed, feeling as fragile as a lily about to snap in the soft warm breeze, Eve took a small step to bring herself into the very male-orientated surroundings of her grandfather's study, and announced. 'If you've both finished playing Russian roulette with my future. I would like to point out that women gained the right to choose for themselves some time during the last century.'

'You break my heart, child,' her grandpa told her painfully. 'I would be failing in my duty to you if I did not make this man formally declare his intentions.'

'He doesn't have any intentions!' Eve slashed at him.

'Yes, I do,' Ethan argued.

She turned on him, eyes burning like phosphorescence as they fixed themselves onto his. His chest swelled, his heart began to pump, other parts of him began to send taunting little signals out across his skin. She was waiting to hear more. More was coming, if he could only get past the sight of her in Galloway's arms.

'Will you marry me, Eve?' There, he'd said it.

'Oh.' She choked, and her eyes filled with tears. 'How could you let him browbeat you into saying that?'

'I didn't.' He was shocked.

'I'll never forgive you for this—never.' She sobbed, turned and ran outside leaving Ethan staring after her in thundering dismay!

'I would go after her if I were you,' Theron smoothly advised while calmly reading the contract Ethan had just signed.

On an act of sheer frustration Ethan snatched the document out of Theron's hands. 'I am sick and tired of other people meddling in my life!' he announced, then turned and walked out of the study—by the conventional route of the door through to the hallway.

Outside he was a mass of offended dignity. Inside he was bubbling with angry offence at the way Eve had rejected him. He'd had enough. Eve was impossible. He was happy to let Aidan Galloway have her. He strode down the hallway with every intention of leaving this house and never stepping foot in it again.

As he crossed the foot of the stairs, he heard a door on the upper landing shut. His feet came to a stop. Bubbling offence had changed to something else entirely, and he knew he wasn't going anywhere but up those stairs to open her shut door.

On a lethal curse, he changed direction. As he took the stairs, two at a time, he had even reached the point of asking how he thought he could walk away, when he could feel that lead still attached to his neck.

She tugged, he went where it pulled him.

Eve stood in the middle of her bedroom and shook from fingers to toes. She couldn't believe he'd said that. She couldn't believe she'd actually looked her dearest in the face then had turned and had walked away from it!

How could he—how *could* he stand there in her grandfather's study wheeling and dealing her life away? He was just like Grandpa: money orientated, power orientated! If she had any sense left she would get out of here. She would disappear somewhere so remote that she would never be found! She hated men—all men. Young, old, they were all the same: arrogant self-obsessed bullies who liked to think they were in control of everything.

The bedroom door suddenly flew open. She spun round to find Ethan standing there. 'If you've come to offer another proposal of marriage then don't bother!' she snapped.

'You will have to get down on your knees to get another one of those out of me,' Ethan grimly returned.

Her knees tried to buckle. Eve felt like screaming. He looked lean and hard, and tough and angry; the bitter expression on his face was spoiling its handsome lines. She liked it. It meant he was hurting. If he was hurting then it had to be because of her—didn't it?

'Then what do you want?' she demanded coldly.

'You,' he said, 'to explain to me what the hell were you doing wrapped in Galloway's arms the moment my back was turned!'

The door slammed shut. Eve's eyes began to fire. 'What were *you* doing leaving me to go to *her*, just because she crooked her little finger at you?' she countered furiously.

Eve folded her arms across her front. Ethan leaned back against the door and did the same. Stalemate. They'd been here before. Excitement began to fizz in the air. Green eyes flashed with it; grey glinted with it. She wanted to go over there and kiss him stupid.

'It was hell,' he pronounced. 'I didn't have any idea how rife the rumours were until I saw the way my arrival was received. I half expected to die the death of a thousand cuts!' He released a short laugh.

'You are still in love with her,' she tossed at him in pained accusation.

'No, I am not,' he tossed right back. 'I am in love with you—God help me!'

'Oh,' she said.

'Yes,' he agreed in grim, tight mockery.

'Then you shouldn't have gone!'

'You should have come. You would have enjoyed the spectacle.'

'You should have invited me.'

'If you hadn't been so pig-stubborn, I probably would have done.'

'Oh,' she said again, and silence settled.

Eve wanted to fill it by throwing herself into his arms and kissing her way back into his good graces. Ethan wanted to fill it by throwing her on that bed he could see across the room and loving her absolutely senseless.

Instead they both looked at the papers he held in his hand. Eve recognised them for what they were; resentment began to flare again.

'Rip it up,' she told him.

'Why?' he asked. 'He's only got me to sign my life away.'

'I don't want your money.'

'I didn't say money, I said life!' He flashed her a hard look. 'Are you telling me you don't want that, either?'

Her chin went up. Two steps and she was snatching the contract from him just as he had snatched it from Theron.

Eve ripped it up. She tossed it to the ground. She placed hands on hips and waited for his eyes to move up from the torn contract to her provocative pose, to her mouth which was wearing its angry pout, and finally to her eyes shot through with challenge. 'Okay,' she announced. 'I'll take your life.'

Ethan reached out, pulled her hard up against him then kissed her... Why not? It was what they both needed. Eve didn't so much as attempt to pull away.

'Now, tell me why were you kissing Aidan Galloway,' he murmured some very satisfying seconds later.

'I wasn't kissing him,' Eve denied. 'I was sobbing on his shoulder because you weren't here and I wanted you to be.'

Ethan brought up a finger to gently touch the corner of her kiss-trembling mouth. 'And the last time I saw you with him like that?' he probed. 'You weren't sobbing then.'

'You misread what you saw that night,' she explained, slid out her tongue and licked his finger and watched as his eyes grew darker in response. 'Aidan had just seen Corin wrapped in a heated clinch with his cousin. They were childhood sweethearts; he's adored her all of his life. He was devastated, I was comforting him when I heard them coming towards us, and I just reacted by kissing Aidan to give Corin a taste of her own nasty medicine.'

'Impulsive as usual.' He sighed.

'Well, you should know.' She flashed. 'When I realised you'd seen us, I knew what you would be thinking. So as soon as I could safely leave Aidan, I *impulsively* went to your room to explain. Only...'

'You found me standing there stark-naked, and decided it was more fun to stare me into embarrassing myself?'

'If that's what you like to think.' She wasn't taking the bait. Instead she caught hold of his finger then fed it across the surface of his own mouth. Already moistened by the tip of her tongue the finger left a film of moisture on his lips.

He licked it off. Sex was suddenly alive in the air. 'You can't control yourself around me,' she informed him smugly, 'which is why you made sure you kept your distance from then on.'

His own hand came to remove her teasing finger. 'You tease and flirt without conscience,' he condemned.

'Your fault,' she blamed. 'The more you disapproved of me the more outrageous I became.'

'Dangerous is the word that comes to my mind.'

He was referring to Raoul Delacroix, Eve realised. It altered the mood so abruptly that Ethan gave a sigh of regret when she withdrew right away from him then walked over to stare out of the bedroom window with her arms crossed over her body in a gesture he recognised as Eve needing to protect Eve.

He followed, unwrapped her arms and replaced them with his own. 'I'm sorry,' he said. 'I didn't mean to resurrect bad memories.'

'I've known Raoul almost all of my life,' she murmured. 'We—all the crowd on the island have been meeting up for holidays there since we were small children. Flirting and teasing was part of the group culture but no one ever took it further than that.'

'But he decided to.'

'We hadn't seen him for a couple of years,' she explained. 'When he came back to the island this summer, he'd changed. We all noticed it, wondered why, but Raoul refused to talk about it. So we drew our own conclusions and decided it had to be a failed love affair or a fall-out with his brother, André, for whom he'd always nurtured a resentment. But never in my wild imaginings did I think he had changed so much that he was capable of pulling something like that.'

'Forget it, it's over.'

'But maybe it was my fault. Maybe I did lead him on.'

'You know that isn't true, so we aren't getting into that,' Ethan said firmly.

Eve pressed back against him and said no more. Beyond the window she watched her grandfather's car taking off down the driveway. The roof was folded away so she could see Aidan sitting next to him. They would be going to a local café where they would drink coffee while Aidan told her grandfather all his woes, and her grandfather would relay wise advice, previously discussed and decided upon with Aidan's older brother, Patrick. It was how it had always worked since Eve had lost her parents and Aidan had lost his in the same car accident, leaving Grandpa to play the role of wise counsellor to both families. Strange really, she mused. But, thinking about it, Raoul had shown signs of resentment to that closeness too.

'Where's your ring?'

Glancing down, she realised that her hands were lost in the clasp of his and his thumb was stroking her naked ring finger in much the same way as her own had been doing every since she'd taken the ring off.

'Tigger has it,' she said.

'And where is Tigger?'

'In my dressing room with his friends.' She went to move. 'Do you want me to go and—?'

'No.' He stopped her. 'We haven't finished here yet.'

'Finished what?' Foolishly she turned in his arms to face him—foolishly, because she should have guessed what was coming, but didn't; so his kiss when it arrived took her breath away.

It was fierce and it was greedy. It brought her hands around his neck and placed his hands on her hip-bones so he could pull her close. She came alive for the first time in too many days to dare think about.

He whispered something into her mouth. 'Marry me,' he said.

'I'm not on my knees.'

'You can go there later. Just say yes.'

'Yes,' she said.

Ethan released a soft laugh. 'Now tell me you love me.' He was going for broke here.

'I love you,' she softly complied.

After that, things moved on a pace. They found the bed, they lost their clothes, Ethan found his little red-painted heart. 'We shouldn't be doing this here,' he thought to remark when it was already way too late. 'This is your grandfather's house. It shows a lack of respect.'

'I don't recall you being so sensitive when you seduced me in Victor Frayne's house,' Eve pointed out.

It more or less put the lid on his conscience so that he could sink himself into what he had started.

Later, much later, they lay in a tangle of satiated limbs. 'You do know I love you to distraction, don't you?' he told her solemnly. 'Leona was—' He stopped, then started the same sentence from a different place. 'I think I only ever loved the idea of loving someone like Leona.' He thought that said it best. 'But in Rahman, when I looked at her, I couldn't even see her face because your beautiful face insisted on imprinting itself over the top of hers. No, don't cry.'

'I'm not crying.' But there were tears in her beautiful eyes, nonetheless. 'I just needed you to say that.'

It cut him to the quick—which he knew he deserved. 'I'm sorry I didn't say it a long time ago.'

She wound her arms around him; he drew her close. They sighed together as their mouths joined. No complicating sex this time, just love and caring and—'

'Get dressed,' he decided suddenly.

'Why?' she protested. Eve was perfectly happy where she was.

'We are going to play the rest of this relationship by the book. So we get dressed, then we will go out and find you something amazing to wear in hot-pink for our official betrothal tonight. Then we get married—next week,' he added as a frowning afterthought. 'Because I don't think we can behave ourselves for longer than that.'

'You won't last a week,' Eve informed him a short ten minutes later as they left her room and his hand was already checking out the smooth line of her bottom.

'I suppose you are going to make it your mission to prove yourself right.'

'Oh, yes,' she said airily. 'I love a good challenge.'

She won, but then she usually did. Eve the flirt, Eve the temptress, went to her marriage bed every night that week.